The Mysteries
of Reverend Dean

The Mysteries
of Reverend Dean

Hal White

Lighthouse
eBooks

To my wife.
You've brought this world
one step closer to heaven.

The Mysteries of Reverend Dean

Published by
Lighthouse Christian Publishing
SAN 257-4330
5531 Dufferin Drive
Savage, Minnesota, 55378
United States of America

www.lighthouseebooks.com
www.lighthousechristianpublishing.com

CONTENTS

Prologue

Outside, the church was small and unimpressive. The cracks in the sidewalk looked like spider webs, beige paint splintered on the south wall, and forest-green moss attacked the roof. The parking lot, also infested with cracks, was too small for the modest church. It held ten cars, while twice that number were parked on the grass of an adjoining field.

Inside, a short, pudgy man — almost, but not quite, bald — perspired as he gripped a worn lectern. He dreaded what he had to do. He didn't doubt his decision — he knew it was time — but it was just the second major change of his life in over thirty years.

And that frightened him.

Almost one hundred listeners fidgeted amidst the silence. Someone coughed. A baby gurgled. The speaker, Reverend Thaddeus Dean, took a sip of tepid water. For the first time in memory, his hands shook. He hoped his congregation wouldn't notice.

"It's unusual for a pastor to be at a loss for words . . . but I find that I am," he said. "As most of you know, after caring for this flock for more than three decades, I am retiring. And except for the death of my beloved wife, Emma, this has been the most difficult experience of my life. The reason it's difficult is because of . . . *you.*"

Heads turned. Eyebrows rose. This wasn't how most retirement sermons ended.

"Yes . . . I lay the blame squarely on your shoulders. Unlike many congregations, who demand much from their pastors but give little in return, the members of this church have encouraged me, comforted me, and held me in prayer on a continual basis. My friends," he asked, spreading his stubby arms as wide as they could go, "how can I easily leave a congregation like that?"

The surprise gave way to sorrow. A sniffle was heard in the back pew. Even the reverend's eyes seemed to moisten.

"Nonetheless, I've always tried to follow my Lord's wishes. And over the past few months I've become convinced this is His will."

The pastor grinned, then continued.

"Regardless of how much I tell Him he's wrong."

The congregation — virtually all of whom Reverend Dean had married, baptized or counseled — beamed at him. He was an institution, but more.

He was loved.

"Nonetheless, I have no idea what I will do next. I hope, at the age of eighty, that my Lord is not yet through with me. So in the meantime, I will bother many of you, at home and at work, while I figure out what to do with my life."

Long-time members laughed. They knew this was no mere threat, particularly if someone was involved in a bizarre or mystifying situation. The old man was a magnet for such events, and over the decades had become something of a local celebrity.

"Here at Outpost Community Church, however, I will only be seen in the congregation." Reverend Dean turned to a handsome, twenty-nine-year-old man sitting next to him. "As of tomorrow, Brother Titus will lead our flock. We are fortunate to have this knowledgeable man as our pastor, and he has my unqualified support and confidence. May he be as blessed by you as I have been."

The cleric turned back to his congregation and paused a final time. His eyes, scanning the sanctuary, stopped briefly on the carpet. It had been installed almost ten years ago, but he still thought of it as new. He glanced at the front entrance. For decades, its massive door had defied every effort to silence its squeak. Looking above, he felt a gentle breeze from the ancient ceiling fans. During his first month as pastor he had horrified Emma by crawling through the rafters to repair them.

But it was the congregation which provided his greatest memories. Each face represented a blend of laughter and sadness, boredom and despair. They were his sheep, and he was their earthly shepherd.

He cleared his throat to speak but, changing his mind, gently shook his head.

"I have many things left to say, but I doubt I could finish them without becoming . . . a bit emotional," he confessed quietly. "Let me just say that, because of you, I am the most blessed of men."

Murder at an Island Mansion

Chapter 1

"I've always wondered, Uncle," asked the pretty twenty-five-year-old, "how did Outpost Community Church get its name? It's in Dark Pine, so why not call it Dark Pine Community Church?"

Thaddeus Dean always enjoyed visits from his relatives, but this call was especially timely. He'd been restless since his retirement as pastor last month, and his beloved Emma had passed away three years ago. Susan's visit was exactly what was needed to lift his spirits.

Although Reverend Dean practiced strict neutrality with all his nieces and nephews, it was hard not to feel a little partial toward Susan. Granted, she lived closer than most relatives — in Seattle, just a two-hour drive from Dark Pine — but that wasn't the reason he appreciated her. Except for Dane, a nephew who also lived in Seattle, Susan was the only relative who called or emailed on a regular basis. She was obviously fond of him. And it didn't hurt that she called him "uncle," rather than emphasizing his age and using his real title: *great* uncle.

"Actually, my dear, I was responsible for *part* of that name," the reverend smiled. "When I arrived in Dark Pine thirty years ago, it was simply called Outpost Church. After years of lobbying, I finally convinced our members to soften the name to Outpost *Community* Church. But to really answer your question, you have to know the history of Dark Pine."

Before continuing, the old man rose from his dilapidated chair and added a log to the fireplace. It was early October and the air had turned chilly. Susan edged closer to the fire, eager for her "history lesson." Uncle Thad had always fascinated her and she loved listening to him. He could describe paint drying, or grass growing, and make it interesting.

Satisfied with the blaze, he shuffled to a window and glanced at the forest near his home. As usual, the night was foggy. Dark Pine ran contrary to what little meteorology the reverend knew. Its gray skies drizzled most of the time, but that didn't prevent waves of fog from rolling down the Cascade Mountains and enveloping the town most nights.

Seeing nothing unusual, he turned from the window. "As you know," he began, "Dark Pine is, and always has been, a town built on lumber and forestry. Situated at the base of the Cascade Range, with its huge forests, I'm sure that doesn't surprise you. What might interest you, however, is that Dark Pine is almost as old as Seattle."

Thaddeus Dean approached his recliner, sat with a heavy thud, and steepled his fingers. "In fact, it was settled by the same people who founded Seattle. Or, I should say, *some* of the same people — because this group left Seattle as a result of an argument with the rest of the settlers."

"What did they argue about?"

"I've wondered that myself," he replied, shaking his head. "All I know is that it happened soon after a vote to build Seattle's first church. Within days, almost ten percent of the settlers headed east to the mountains, and founded Dark Pine.

"Except for selling lumber to nearby towns, Dark Pine remained fairly isolated. This was apparently the choice of the people who lived here. Eventually, however, one pastor felt called to start a church in the area. By all accounts he was a rough, tough-minded individual. Which was fortunate, because Dark Pine was a rough town, and it didn't want a church.

"Nonetheless, the frontier pastor prevailed and founded Dark Pine's first place of worship. From the beginning, however, he felt isolated and besieged. Isolated physically, because it took a lot longer to get to Seattle then than it does now, and besieged spiritually. The longer he lived here, the more he believed there were influences working against Christ that he'd never encountered anywhere else. So he named the church Outpost Church, to reflect his belief that he was waging a battle at a lonely outpost on the fringe of Christian influence."

"You make Dark Pine sound almost evil."

"Those were his words, not mine," he reminded her. "But I believe he . . . *may* have had a point." His face turned somber.

"Whatever do you mean, Uncle?"

He shrugged, in an effort to downplay his concern. "Over the decades, a believer sometimes develops a . . . discernment, for lack of a better word, towards certain events," the old man answered cryptically. "In Dark Pine I have felt things — and seen things — that are . . . unusual."

To his dismay he saw a look of apprehension creep onto Susan's face. He immediately leaned forward and took her hand in his stubby fingers. "My dear, my comments have disturbed you. I'm so sorry. You asked about Outpost's history, and I fear I've told you more than you wished to know."

He scanned her with large, worried eyes, berating himself for being insensitive to a cherished guest.

"Oh, pooh," replied Susan, much to his relief. "I'm not as delicate as you think, Uncle. I live on Capitol Hill, remember? I've seen weirder things than you'll *ever* see in Dark Pine."

Both smiled at Susan's attempt to lighten the mood, as well as her reference to Seattle's most bohemian neighborhood.

"But I *should* be getting to bed," she admitted. "I have to drive back early tomorrow morning."

Susan had spent the night several times, so formalities were suspended as Reverend Dean unrolled a sleeping bag on the study floor. When he eventually turned in — never before 2 AM, because he was an incorrigible night owl — he would sleep there.

Susan, for her part, reviewed the bed in her uncle's bedroom. The first time she'd visited after Aunt Emma died, Reverend Dean had forgotten to change the sheets. She'd slept in the bed, of course, but later gently suggested that clean linen was appreciated by any guest. They'd laughed about the incident several times over the years.

"Good night, Uncle," she said, giving him a hug. "I'll make my own breakfast tomorrow. I know you hate to get up early," she teased.

The old man grinned, but didn't object. They both knew he wasn't an early riser. More than once he'd claimed that sleeping late was the best part of retirement.

Long after Susan went to bed, Reverend Dean stared into the fire, thinking and wondering about Dark Pine.

He checked the door locks twice before going to bed.

Chapter 2

Reverend Dean awoke at the crack of ten, stretched, and groggily crawled out of his sleeping bag. He stumbled toward the kitchen, fumbled with his overworked coffeemaker, and — miraculously, because his eyes were virtually shut — deposited the proper amount of water and Slow Roast into the machine. Rubbing sleep from his eyes, he picked up a note left by Susan.

Thanks for dinner, Uncle Thad! I'll see you next month!
Love, Susan.

The old man smiled. No one else in the world called him Thad. What a delightful girl. He placed the note gently on the counter, pulled his favorite mug from the shelf — purchased by Emma at Starbucks, although the logo had long since worn off — and filled it with coffee. He was on his way to greet Puppadawg, his ancient St. Bernard, when the phone rang.

"Reverend! Hello! This is Vicky Calais. I'm glad I caught you. Do you have a minute?"

It took him a moment to identify the caller. Vicky Calais was the daughter of Robert Calais, a former member of the church. Several years ago he'd inherited a mansion on a small island in

Puget Sound, and wasted little time in moving Vicki and her four siblings to the estate. Vicki's mother, if the reverend's memory served (and it always did), died somewhat mysteriously after moving to the island. As time passed, Reverend Dean lost touch with the family. However, he remembered Vicki as an energetic, fourteen-year-old girl. He abruptly realized that she must be eighteen by now. The old man shook his head. How time flies.

"Vicki, it's delightful to hear from you. Of course I have a minute. How are you? How is your father?"

A pause revealed that all was not well with Vicki's father.

"Reverend . . . he died last month," she replied in a small voice.

"Vicki, I am so sorry, my child. How did it happen, if I might ask?"

"It was a stroke, Reverend. It happened very suddenly, although he lingered for almost a week." The young caller paused. "I suppose it might have been a blessing, actually. I loved him, and miss him horribly, but many stroke victims survive as vegetables. At least Daddy didn't suffer like that."

"I'm sorry I wasn't there to help you, Vicki," he replied sincerely. "It must have been very difficult for you."

"It was, Reverend. In fact, one of the reasons I called is because you know what it's like to lose a loved one."

The old man hesitated. "Yes," he said quietly.

"But there's a second reason I wanted to talk to you." The young woman paused before continuing. "Reverend, do you believe in ghosts?"

He couldn't have been more surprised if she'd asked if he believed in flying brooms. Nonetheless, given last night's discussion — and the proximity to Halloween — it seemed oddly appropriate. In any event, he knew by the sound of Vicki's voice that she was serious. Like any good counselor, he sought to clarify the question before responding.

"What do you mean by 'ghost'?"

"You know, spirits of dead people; haunting places before they go to heaven or hell."

Reverend Dean considered his response. Whatever the cause of such events — demons, unknown natural phenomena, or wishful thinking — he didn't believe that some souls became "lost" *en route* to their final destination, or stayed behind to complete "unfinished business." That implied souls had self-determination regarding where they went after death, and that was unbiblical.[1] He remembered Vicki as a strong, rational girl, so he decided to be frank in his response.

"I think it unlikely," he replied. "That's not to say I don't believe in the supernatural. I do. However, whatever causes sounds in the night — or even apparitions — I doubt the explanation lies with disoriented souls. If there's an afterlife, then there's assuredly a God; and if there's a God, I doubt He would permit souls to go astray."

"Then . . . then I must be going mad!" the young woman wailed.

Obviously the situation was worse than he realized. "My child, tell me what's happened."

The question seemed to calm and focus the girl, albeit slightly. "Reverend, I hardly know where to start. But I suppose . . . I suppose it began in the hospital, when Daddy was dying."

Vicki took a deep breath, composed her thoughts, and continued. "Daddy had been hospitalized for about a week and was fading fast. He was conscious, but not doing well. Everyone had been in and out of the room to see him—"

"Who, exactly, my child?"

"Well, Zach, Rachel, Jay, Leon, Mary . . . and of course me. They wouldn't let anyone else in."

He recognized four names as Vicki's siblings, but one wasn't familiar. "Who is Mary?" he asked.

"She's my best friend. We met at the University of Washington. We have different majors — she's in physical education, I'm in drama — but every freshman has to take philosophy, so we met there. In fact, after I invited her to spend a week at the estate, Dad was so taken with Mary that he let her live with us."

"Ah, your father was . . . *taken* with her?"

The girl chuckled. "Don't worry, Reverend, it wasn't like that. Mary was like a daughter to him. Believe me, I know. I live there. Besides, she has a boyfriend."

"Ah," he smiled. "Of course. Pray continue."

"Well, the afternoon that Daddy died, I walked into his hospital room and found. . ." Vicki paused to collect herself. "Reverend, I found footprints leading from his bed to the window!"

"Footprints? Of what?"

"Of feet."

The reverend smiled. "Of course, my child, but what substance caused the footprints? Water? Mud. . ."

"Oh, I'm sorry. How silly. Mud. The footprints were of mud. They ran from his bed to the wall, *up* the wall, and onto the windowsill."

"How odd. Was the window open?"

"No. It was the modern type that didn't open. It was also on the third floor, if that makes any difference."

"Peculiar," he mumbled. "Could anyone explain these footprints?"

"No, and no one had seen them before, either. But there's more. I also found a note clutched in Dad's hand."

"Written by whom?"

"By Dad, although his handwriting was pretty shaky toward

the end, as you might imagine. It was the last thing he ever wrote. He never regained consciousness afterward. He died . . . that evening."

"I know this is difficult for you, Vicki," he sympathized. After a pause, he gently asked, "Can you tell me what the note said?"

"Reverend, now it starts to get weird. I mean, except for the footprints, which were also weird. The note read:

Footprints will carry me away,
but no seller of my house
will see any footprints
before he dies.

"Do those words mean anything to you?" he inquired.

"No. And they don't mean anything to anyone else, either. I mean, Dad didn't want the house sold, but he left that decision up to us; or up to Zach, at any rate."

"What do you mean?"

"Well, Dad didn't want any fighting regarding what would happen to the mansion. So in his will he left sole power to sell the estate to the oldest child. That's Zach. Of course, if the estate is sold we'll share all the proceeds equally, but the actual decision was Zach's, and he wanted to sell."

Reverend Dean picked up on the past tense. "'Wanted?'"

"Zach. . ." The girl began to cry. "Oh, Reverend, Zach was murdered two weeks ago!"

Reverend Dean was stunned. "There, there, my child. . ." he murmured, as the woman sobbed.

Eventually, after two minutes, Vicki regained her composure.

"How did it happen, my dear?"

"That's what's so bizarre!" she said bitterly. "The mansion is a waterfront estate, and just before he was murdered Zach said he was going down to the beach to read. Twenty minutes later he received a phone call at the mansion. He didn't respond to my yells — even though I could see him lying on the sand — so I was pretty annoyed when I had to walk down to get him. But Reverend, when I got there, Zach had been. . ." Vicki paused to stifle a sob, "Zach had been stabbed! He was dead!"

Vicki's crying, previously in check, began anew. Reverend Dean couldn't imagine how difficult this was for her. He waited patiently until she composed herself.

"What did the police say?" he asked gently.

"That's the strange thing — or the *next* strange thing, I should say. The police are clueless. Not only that, I think they suspect me!"

"You? Why?"

"Reverend, there were no footprints around Zach's body — not even his own! The only tracks were mine, when I walked down to tell him about the call! It's just what was written in Dad's note: *no seller of my house will see any footprints before he dies!*"

"But surely there are explanations. . ." The reverend's keen mind began to work. "Someone could have approached Zach from the water, or someone could have brushed the sand smooth as he retreated from the body. . ."

"No, Reverend, they couldn't. It had been raining earlier that day. The sand was wet, and couldn't be brushed to conceal footprints. And Zach was lying a good twenty feet from the shore. No one could have approached him without leaving prints."

Reverend Dean was stumped. "My child, I am so sorry. What would you like me to do?"

"Come visit us, Reverend. I've spoken to Rachel and Jay, and they would like to see you. We know you have experience in things like . . . like this, and we're all . . . we're all *scared*. Will you come?"

Vicki's omission of Leon didn't go unnoticed by Reverend

Dean. Nevertheless, the other children desired his presence, and he was definitely intrigued. More importantly, these children — now adults — had grown up in his church. He felt a responsibility toward them.

"It would be an honor to visit you, Vicki. When shall I come?"

"Oh, thank you, Reverend! Come as soon as possible! Rachel's the oldest now. And she. . ."

"She *what*, my child?"

"She wants to sell the estate too! Please hurry!"

Chapter 3

The trip to Seattle was uneventful. Reverend Dean drove his car onto the ferry, parked and locked the vehicle, then climbed to the boat's upper deck. Strolling toward the front of the ship he leaned against the railing, closed his eyes, and smiled.

As a lover of everything aquatic, Reverend Dean always enjoyed a ferry ride. Especially if it was raining. Water above and water below; what more could he possibly want? Unfortunately, the day was distressingly sunny. Still, any boat ride was special for him.

Several years ago he read an article which listed various things each state was "best" at. He couldn't remember the whole list, but he recalled a few things at which Washington excelled: the best airplanes (which was no surprise, due to Boeing); the best apples; the best salmon; and — gratifyingly — the best ferry system.

As Reverend Dean examined the boat he made a mental note to visit Washington's — and as far as he knew, the world's — only art deco ferry. Christened in 1935, the *Kalakala* was unique, looking more like a plane without wings than a ferry. The boat had been rescued from an obscure, rusting grave, and gently tugged back to Puget Sound. The last he'd heard it was undergoing an uncertain restoration — due to limited funds — in Tacoma. He hoped the effort succeeded. There was nothing remotely like it in the world.[2]

As the ferry approached its destination, Reverend Dean tried to recall what he knew about Manor Island. It was sparsely populated, and it probably wouldn't be on the ferry line at all if it weren't for the surprising number of mansions and estates on the island. They'd been built by old money — old by Seattle standards, at least — and all save one were still used as homes by the original owners' descendants.

The lone exception was now a museum and it — along with a smattering of artists' boutiques — comprised what little economy the island had. There was a small elementary school and a volunteer fire brigade; but no police force, church or library. In fact there was no town, as such. Technically it was a part of unincorporated San Juan County, a collection of islands in Washington's Puget Sound.

As the ferry docked, Reverend Dean retreated to his dilapidated Ford and maneuvered carefully off the boat. Vicki had emailed a map of the island, and after fifteen minutes he found himself driving through the open gates of *Chez Calais*. As he crept past a large expanse of lawn and approached the mansion, he expected to be greeted by Vicki.

Instead he was met by three cars owned by the San Juan County Sheriff's Department.

Reverend Dean parked on the far side of the driveway and approached the house. Halfway to the mansion Vicki burst through a side door.

"Oh, Reverend, thank goodness you're here! It's been horrible! Horrible!"

"There, there, my child," the reverend soothed, holding the weeping girl. "What's happened?"

"Reverend, Rachel's been murdered! Stabbed, just like Zach!

But no one could have done it! It's impossible! Impossible!" she sobbed. The girl was hysterical. "It must be a ghost! It must be!" she wailed.

Reverend Dean held Vicki firmly by her shoulders and looked in her eyes. "Vicki," he said with gentle firmness. "Vicki, *listen* to me, my child. Do not lose hope. There is an explanation for this tragedy and, God willing, we will find it. Now let's walk inside and you can tell me the details."

Calmed by the reverend's composure, the old man and young woman walked slowly to the mansion's side door. They were met by several departing officers.

"Who're you?" the lead detective demanded, jutting his chin toward Reverend Dean.

"A friend of the family," replied the reverend.

"He's our pastor," Vicki explained.

The burly sheriff gave Reverend Dean a quick exam, grunted, and led his men out the door. The old man watched them depart, and cocked an eyebrow.

"Not the warmest officer I've met," he observed drily.

"Like I said, I think he suspects *me*," Vicki explained bitterly. "Let's go in the kitchen, Reverend. I'll fix some coffee."

As the troubled girl set about her task, the reverend couldn't help but notice how she'd changed. A blonde, pudgy-cheeked adolescent had grown into a willowy, fashionably-dressed coed. As he examined the room a silent figure materialized in the doorway.

"Reverend, you remember Leon," introduced Vicki.

It would have been hard to forget Leon. The man was huge, at least six foot three and two hundred fifty pounds. But that wasn't his most prominent feature. In addition to his size, Leon had long black hair and a beard that traveled past his collar. If Reverend Dean had seen anyone with a closer likeness to Rasputin, the mad Russian monk, he couldn't remember it. The old man smiled and extended his hand.

Leon stared at the hand then turned to Vicki. "The cops said they'll call us when they need us," he said gruffly. "I'm still trying to find Jay."

Vicki acknowledged her brother's comments with a nod. Leon glanced at their guest. "Reverend," he mumbled, leaving the kitchen.

"I take it Leon doesn't approve of my visit," he asked frankly.

The girl grabbed two mugs and paused. "No," she replied honestly, "he doesn't. Leon thinks the whole affair should be kept between the family and the police. He's also become a militant atheist. So, to Leon, you already have two strikes against you."

The girl poured coffee into the mugs, handed one to Reverend Dean, and sat down. "But he's a gentle giant. He's very protective of me, and in some ways he's my favorite brother." Tears formed in the girl's eyes. "Of the ones who are left, anyway."

"There, there, my child," said the reverend, patting her arm, "why don't you tell me what happened today?"

The girl sniffled as she collected her thoughts. "Like I told you on the phone, Rachel wanted to sell the house. She is — or was — the next oldest after Zach, so she had the power to make that decision. Jay agreed with her. So they decided to spruce up the estate in anticipation of selling it. Rachel's project was to paint the upstairs rooms, and Jay was going to drain a retaining pond next to the house. It's true that both jobs needed to be done but, as you may have guessed, I don't want to leave here.

"Anyway, that's where Rachel was this morning: painting the upstairs guest room. Around noon I heard an awful scream. I was in the kitchen, so I rushed upstairs. Leon heard the yell too, and we met at the guest room door."

The girl became visibly agitated. "But here's where it gets impossible, Reverend! Rachel was sitting on the floor in the far corner of the room, with a knife in her back! The entire room was empty, because she was painting it. But instead of paint on the walls, there was paint all over the floor! Not spilled, mind you, but brushed! She had painted the entire hardwood floor! The only part that wasn't painted was the corner she was sitting in!"

"But why do you say a ghost must have done it, my child?"

"Reverend, less than ten seconds had passed before Leon and I were at the bedroom door. When we ran in the room, we realized the paint on the floor was fresh — it wasn't even partly dry. But there were no footprints, just like before! No one could leave the room that quickly without leaving footprints! I came from the downstairs, and Leon came from the other end of the upstairs. No one passed us! But even if they did, how could they do it without leaving footprints? The floor was wet! With poor Rachel lying in the corner with a knife in her!"

"Vicki, I'm sorry to interrupt," the reverend apologized, "but where were the paint and paintbrush?"

Vicki closed her eyes, recreating the scene in her mind. "Next to Rachel. In the unpainted corner of the room."

The old man frowned as he recalled the words of the father's note. *No seller of my house will see any footprints before he dies.* "I'd like to see the room, if I may," he asked gently.

"Of course, Reverend. Follow me."

The unlikely pair left the kitchen, traveled through the dining room with its enormous chandelier, and ascended an antique, grand staircase. Reverend Dean marveled at its opulence. He'd never seen such craftsmanship outside of museums or photographs. But given the elegance of the mansion, it seemed entirely appropriate. They arrived quickly at the second of three floors, rounded a corner, and walked to the first doorway. The old man noticed two pairs of shoes at the entrance. Vicki followed his eyes.

"We took off our shoes, so we wouldn't track paint through the house," the girl explained sensibly. "But you can go in now. The paint's dry."

Reverend Dean did so. The scene was as macabre as Vicki described. There were two sets of footprints leading to the far corner of the room, which consisted of an unpainted area roughly four feet square. The walls were bare on all sides, except for a closet on the same side of the room as the door, and a window next to the closet. Reverend Dean estimated the distance between the unpainted corner and the window. It was at least ten feet. No one could have leapt from the corner to the window — much less to the door — without leaving some kind of trace in the wet paint.

To Vicki's surprise, the old pastor got down on his hands and knees and examined the floor of the room. After he rose, he walked to the window and peered outside. There was no roof or ledge to hide or rest upon. In fact, the only thing close to the window was a small tree branch, which the reverend predicted would break if he were to jump onto it.

Which — given the four-foot leap, and twelve-foot drop to the ground — he had no intention of doing.

Finally he inspected the closet. After noting that one of the sliding doors was off its track, he rose and peered at his hostess.

"Where did your brother come from, exactly?" he asked.

Vicki walked out of the room and pointed down the hall. "Leon's a writer," she explained, "so he's usually in the far room at the end of the hallway, where it's the quietest. That's where he was all morning."

The reverend peered down the corridor and back to the guest room, making silent calculations in his head. Vicki said nothing because she was mesmerized by the old man's eyes. She recalled a TV show where a comic had made fun of people whose 'lights were on, but no one was home.'

She gazed at Reverend Dean's eyes. Someone was home in there, all right. There was no doubt about that. She almost jumped when the old man finally spoke.

"Vicki, would you show me the grounds?" he asked kindly.

"Of course, Reverend. Follow me."

Vicki led them out the kitchen door. It appeared the front door was seldom used.

"Where to first?" the young woman inquired.

"Let's look underneath the guest room window."

Upon arriving at that spot, Reverend Dean examined the ground, the tree and the side of the house. Although he said nothing, Vicki was pretty sure that he was disappointed.

"If it's not too painful, Vicki," the old man gently asked, "would you show me where Zach was killed?"

"Of course, Reverend. It's this way."

As they descended to the beach, Reverend Dean pointed to a muddy depression in the ground. It was roughly the circumference of his house in Dark Pine.

"Was that the retaining pond?"

"Yes. Actually, I'm glad to be rid of it. They're such an eyesore, don't you think?"

Reverend Dean wanted to be diplomatic, but he felt strongly on the issue. Water, in all its forms, appealed to him.

"They don't have to be," he suggested. "I've seen some retaining ponds which were very attractive. They just need the right plants along the edges, and enough time to develop an ecosystem." The old pastor shrugged and smiled at the same time. "Aren't you glad you asked?" he teased.

Vicki smiled back. The reverend had a way of disagreeing that wasn't in the least bit disagreeable. He also had a point. No one had made any effort to cultivate the pond. Vicki walked several more steps and pointed to a spot on the beach.

"That's where I found Zach," she said quietly.

Reverend Dean scanned the area. It was just as Vicki had described on the phone. Approximately twenty feet from the shoreline — even further at low tide, he observed — and at least that far from the shrubbery line. All in all, there was approximately forty feet of nothing but sand and the occasional rock, stump, or sea shell. But even those objects were never clustered together, always five or more feet apart. Reverend Dean shook his head in annoyance at the apparently insoluble murder. Even if someone were a champion broad jumper, there were no objects large enough to land on. He was no closer to a solution than before he arrived.

Actually, he was further away, because now he had a *second* impossible crime: the murder of poor Rachel. The only common denominator was Vicki. But if she were involved, why would she send for him? To be some sort of alibi? Or witness? But of what?

The old man considered another alternative. Leon clearly didn't want him snooping around, and he was admittedly on the same floor as Rachel when she was murdered. But how had he done it? How could *anyone* have killed Rachel without leaving a trace, and vanish mere seconds before witnesses arrived? The old man sighed and looked at his hostess.

"I think it's time for me to think," the old man admitted. "Could I rest in my room for a bit, Vicki?"

"Of course, Reverend. It's all ready for you. Dinner's at seven, although I doubt it'll be very lively tonight."

The young girl stifled a sob, and led the pastor to his room.

Chapter 4

As predicted, dinner began on a somber note. The dark, hulking Leon ate swiftly, said little, and quickly departed. Only after his exit, as Vicki served desert, did the mood lighten.

"Well, Reverend," Jay began, "I'd apologize for my younger brother, but I'm sure you remember how he is. Now that we can talk, what do you make of our little troubles here?"

Reverend Dean examined the eldest of the remaining children. Jay was shorter and less muscular than Leon — painfully thin, in fact — and his blond hair contrasted sharply with his brother's black curls. Were it not for a facial likeness it would be hard to imagine they were siblings. Their personalities were also different. Leon was dour and taciturn, while Jay was jolly and cynical. But that didn't surprise the reverend. Each of the Calais children possessed markedly different personalities.

"*Jay!* How can you call the murder of Zach and Rachel a 'little trouble!'" Vicki exclaimed, slamming her fork on the table.

"I'm sorry, sis. You know what I mean. . ."

Vicki looked away and nodded, reluctantly accepting Jay's apology. Seeking to change the subject, Reverend Dean turned to Vicki's friend.

"Mary, Vicki is fortunate to have you during this tragic time.

Does your family live in the area?"

The short, stocky girl hesitated, then — judging from her expression — decided to be candid. "My parents died when I was less than a year old. I was raised by my grandparents in Idaho. My grandfather died of a heart attack a decade ago, and my grandmother died of pneumonia last year. So, to answer your question," Mary spread her arms around the table, "this is the only family I have."

Rarely had Reverend Dean felt so embarrassed after asking a question. Fortunately, the girl showed no offense. He saw why Vicki and her father enjoyed her company. Mary had a polite, charming demeanor, even when answering a stranger's question about personal tragedies.

The old man hastily changed the subject. "Mary, I'm . . . very sorry to hear that. Was it your grandmother's desire that you attend the University of Washington?"

"Very much so," the pretty girl beamed. "She didn't have enough money to send me to college so, when the U.W. offered a scholarship, we were both relieved."

"Mary's on the gymnastics team," Vicki explained, with vicarious pride.

"I'm sure your grandparents would be very pleased," the old man smiled.

"Reverend, now that you know all about *us*," interrupted Jay, "I'm still waiting for you to bring your famous powers to bear on our little—" he glanced at Vicki, then corrected himself, "uh, on the tragedies we've suffered around here."

Reverend Dean adroitly sidestepped the young man's question. "Actually, Jay, I don't know what *you've* been up to lately. The last time we spoke, you were still in college."

The older brother shrugged. "Not much to tell, really. After I graduated, I decided to work for Dad. You remember the auto dealership he owned in Dark Pine? Well, after he sold that company, he used the proceeds to buy a new dealership in Bremerton. By the time he died he owned a total of three dealerships."

"Will you manage all of them?"

"Well, originally I was going to manage one, Zach one, and Rachel one, but obviously that can't happen now." He turned to Vicki's friend. "What about you, Mary? Leon would rather write, and Vicki's not interested."

Mary knew that Jay was teasing her, so she blushed, smiled at her plate, and silently mouthed the word, "No." Jay winked at the reverend with an expression that said, "Hey, I offered."

It seemed to Reverend Dean that with the exception of Leon, the house got along well together. Now that the conversation was flowing, he was reluctant to change the subject. Nonetheless, he felt compelled to do so.

"Jay, I don't mean to intrude, but I'm curious to know what you intend to do with the estate. As I understand it, with the death of Zach and Rachel, you're the oldest and the decision is yours."

"That's no mystery, Reverend. With most of our family gone — Mom, Dad, Zach, and now Rachel — it's simply no longer practical for three," he nodded toward Mary, "or even four people to live here. So I plan to sell it. The sooner the better."

"*Excuse* me," said Vicki bitterly, as she pushed back her chair and stomped to the kitchen.

"Even if some don't agree?" the reverend asked, nodding toward Vicki's empty chair.

Jay sighed in exasperation. "It isn't like we haven't talked about it, Reverend, but Vicki's not a businessman. It makes no financial sense to maintain this mansion. She'll thank me, eventually." Jay looked toward the kitchen. "Anyway, it's been a long day, and tomorrow I have to arrange the details of Rachel's funeral. I think I'll make an early night of it. I'll see you tomorrow, Reverend, Mary."

Vicki peered out the kitchen door as Jay departed. "That Jay! I love him dearly, but you'd think Rachel's death would make him think twice about selling the estate. At least until we catch whoever — or whatever — killed her and Zach." She wrung both hands on her apron and started to cry. "Oh, Reverend, can't you talk some sense into him?"

The old man shook his head. "I'm afraid family finances are beyond my purview," he said. He sympathized with Vicki, but he knew this was none of his business.

"However, I do agree with Jay on one matter," he allowed. "It makes sense to get a good night's sleep. Vicki, I thank you for a superb dinner; and for your and Mary's delightful company. But an old man knows his limitations," he smiled, "and I've reached mine. I'll see you both tomorrow."

"Good night, Reverend. At least tomorrow can't be as bad as today."

Try as he might, Reverend Thaddeus Dean couldn't sleep. He'd brought his white-noise machine — a small device that supposedly sounded like rain, but really sounded like static — and dutifully plugged it into an outlet. Once, when the electricity had failed in Dark Pine, he had tried to sleep without the calming noise. It had been utterly impossible. After using it for years to mask sounds, he was incapable of sleeping without it.

Still, even with his acoustic security blanket, he could not sleep.

As he stared at the dark ceiling, his mind returned over and over to the same questions. Why would Rachel paint the floor? And were the deaths really related to the sale of the house? That had been Vicki's assumption, but was it correct? And what about the father? Was his death as natural as it appeared, or had he been murdered too? He'd wanted to spare the children more grief, so he hadn't raised that possibility. But it had to be considered.

Frequently, insights came to the old man while he lay in bed. Tonight, all he received were more questions. Hours later he drifted into a reluctant, half-hearted sleep.

Chapter 5

"Vicki! Vicki! Come here! Hurry! *Hurry!*"

Reverend Dean had just turned off his noisemaker when he heard Mary's screams. Throwing on his clothes, he rushed downstairs and immediately noticed that the patio door was open. Looking outside he saw Mary and Vicki running toward the center of the muddy retaining pond. As he pursued the girls he saw what alarmed them.

A body was lying in the center of the mud.

Mary reached the body first, with Vicki a few steps behind. As Reverend Dean joined the frantic girls he looked down at the unfortunate victim — and was met by the vacant stare of Jay.

It was vacant because a knife protruded from his heart.

The reverend saw something else, as well. There were no tracks leading up to the body except those of Mary, Vicki and himself.

Vicki noticed this too. "Reverend! How? How could this *happen*!? There are no tracks, just like before! What's happening!? *What's happening*!?" The girl grabbed him so fiercely that he feared they might fall in the mud. But even as he struggled to keep them erect, he had no explanation. He had never felt so frustrated.

Leon, attracted by the commotion, ran to the group. After a

brief glance at the body, he retreated to the mansion and called the sheriff. Judging from his expression, he was as frustrated and angry as everyone else.

By the time the police and coroner left — several hours later — the detectives appeared to mistrust everyone in the house. Vicki was the main suspect because she had no alibi for any of the murders, and was the person who had found Zach. Leon — who had no alibis, either — also drew suspicion due to his wild appearance and overall demeanor.

And *both* siblings, the police discovered, wanted to keep the house, thus providing motive.

Nor did the police ignore Mary or Reverend Dean. Unfortunately — from the perspective of the police, at least — Mary had no motive to kill anyone, and Reverend Dean wasn't even on the island when Rachel and Zach were murdered. As a result, the detectives focused on Vicki with a vengeance. Reverend Dean spent an hour consoling the girl after the authorities left. Her emotions ran the gamut from hysteria to despair to — ultimately — exhaustion.

It was during that time, while holding the distraught girl's hand and quietly staring out the patio door, that Reverend Dean understood how the crimes had been committed.

And who committed them.

Unfortunately, he could think of only one way to prove his theory. It would be risky, but there was no alternative. After a quick prayer, he gently held Vicki by the shoulders. "My child, it's way past dinner time. Why don't we get something to eat? Would you like that?"

"I won't eat in this horrid house! I won't!"

"Of course not. I understand. Is there a nearby restaurant we can go to?"

Leon entered the room and overheard the reverend's question.

"There's a diner by the ferry terminal," he said gruffly. "We can go there. I'll get Mary."

The prospect of action — any action — seemed to lighten Vicki's mood. Reverend Dean gently urged her from the sofa as Leon and Mary descended the stairs. Before the quartet made its way to the garage, Reverend Dean silently pocketed an object from the living room.

No one spoke during the short drive to the restaurant. As the foursome entered the diner and approached a booth, Reverend Dean made sure he faced Leon on the outside of the table, with the woman facing each other on the inside.

The quartet made a pretense of studying the menus, gave orders to a bored, middle-aged waitress, then stared mutely at the red, laminated table. Vicki's eyes were still moist.

"I can't return your siblings, Vicki, but I can do one thing for you," the reverend began softly. "I can, at least, lay to rest the fear that you're persecuted by a ghost. It was no ghost that killed Zach, Rachel or Jay. It was someone sitting at this table."

All eyes focused on Reverend Dean. Leon, sitting across from the cleric, seemed threatening. Vicki, adjacent to the old man, looked stunned. Mary, merely sad.

"Each murder provided a clue," he began gently. "Specifically, the *way* each murder was accomplished."

"But we don't *know* how they were accomplished!" Vicki wailed, on the verge of crying again.

"But we do, my child," the old man soothed, "we do."

"*How?*" Leon snarled.

The reverend eyed the man evenly. "Zach's murder, on a wet beach, many feet from shore, was accomplished this way."

He unscrewed the tops off a saltshaker, peppershaker and catsup bottle, and placed each of them five inches apart on the table. He then took a pencil from his pocket, placed one end on the salt top, and the other end on the catsup top.

"As you'll recall, there were scattered pieces of driftwood and large shells along the beach," he began. "The murderer ambushed Zach on his way to the beach and knocked him unconscious. Then the murderer placed one end of a long, narrow board — perhaps a two-by-four — on one large shell, and the other end on a stump of driftwood, approximately five feet distant. The murderer carried Zach across the board, pivoted the board onto a further piece of driftwood, ferried Zach across this distance, and finally laid him onto the sand."

Reverend Dean pivoted the end of his pencil from the salt top to the pepper top, then picked up a knife — representing Zach — and gently laid it on the table. No one spoke. Everyone was stunned.

"The second murder was equally well planned, and involved a skillful misdirection of time. As we all know, on the day she died, Rachel went upstairs to paint the guest bedroom. Tragically, she was murdered as soon as she entered the room."

"But the paint—"

"The paint was brushed on the floor *after* Rachel had been murdered and placed in the corner of the room. The murderer started painting at the door, then painted down to and around poor Rachel. At that point, the murderer poured some paint into a disposable container, set the original paintbrush and can next to the body, and used a second brush to literally paint him or herself into a corner at the far window. The murderer then opened the window, sat on the sill, and painted the remaining portion of the floor. After tossing the extra brush and paint into a bag, and making a horrible scream — which you thought was Rachel — the murderer closed the window and jumped onto the tree branch several feet away. Of course, from that spot — if necessary — it would have taken just seconds to reenter the house."

The reverend paused, and looked at Vicki and Mary.

"But you see where this leaves us. Only a woman could have impersonated Rachel's scream. And only a woman could have hung from that narrow tree branch. If Leon had grabbed that limb, it would have snapped off the tree."

Leon looked relieved, but said nothing. Both women, however, immediately filled the booth with protests.

Reverend Dean held up both hands to instill order. "Please, allow me to finish. I promise I'll be brief.

"The third murder was choreographed so that it could only work from a certain angle. That angle was from the patio door, which looked directly onto the former pond. The murderer knocked Jay unconscious, carried him to the middle of the mud flat, stabbed him, and then slowly retreated, stepping backward into her own footprints."

Reverend Dean looked directly at Mary, who stared defiantly back.

"After you'd retraced your steps halfway back, you called out to Vicki. She rushed to the living room, and from the perspective of the patio door she could see you, but couldn't see the steps you'd made in front of you. She naturally assumed that you'd gone halfway to the body, identified it as Jay, then called out before proceeding further. Once Vicki began to run to the pond, you ran forward as well, stepping into your previous footprints. This gave Vicki the impression that your steps were made simultaneously with hers."

Unable to speak, Vicki turned toward Mary in horror. Leon, clenching his massive hands into fists, glared demonically at the girl.

However, Mary's expression abruptly changed to the wholesome, gracious demeanor which had enchanted Reverend Dean the night before.

"Reverend, this is quite a joke you're playing, but I know you're just pulling my leg," she said pleasantly. "Not only was I with my boyfriend when Rachel died, but I don't see how you can prove any of this."

The girl smiled coyly at the pastor, but the old man was unimpressed.

"I'm sorry, Mary, but your performance won't work anymore. Regarding your supposed alibi, you merely killed Rachel before you met your boyfriend. That will be easy enough to establish. Regarding proof, it's what we discussed last night that provided the clue to this puzzle. Vicki said you were a gymnast; and not just any gymnast, but one so adept that you received a scholarship."

The old man turned toward the siblings. "Recall how each murder was carried out. The first included walking on a narrow board, which uses the exact skill needed for a balance beam. The second required leaping onto a tree branch, which employs the same talent needed for the uneven bars. And the final murder, where steps were retraced, used the precise, rapid foot movement required when performing floor routines."

"*There isn't any proof, you stupid old man!*"

Reverend Dean slowly turned toward Mary. "Do you remember when I said the final murder could only be accomplished if it were viewed at a certain angle?"

Mary's indignation changed to uncertainty.

"Did you also notice that, directly overlooking the retaining pond, there is a ventilation grill in the attic?"

The color drained from Mary's face.

"The problem with committing murders where footprints normally appear, is that there are few places where that naturally occurs. And the only remaining place I could imagine being used was the retaining pond. Fortunately, the vents provided an excellent vantage point for a video camera."

"You're . . . you're bluffing."

Reverend Dean reached in his pocket, slowly pulled out a videotape, and laid it gently on the table. "It's the type that's used in old-style video recorders," he confessed, "not all of us can afford small digital cams."

The old man paused. "It's over, my child."

Mary considered making a dash from the booth, but with the hulking Leon on one side, and a wall on the other, any attempt was hopeless. Sensing Mary's intent, it suddenly occurred to Leon why Reverend Dean had maneuvered him to the outside of the booth.

Mary looked apologetically at Vicki. "I never would've hurt you, Vicki. Please believe that. Or you, Leon." The girl slumped in the booth, and turned toward the wall. "It's a relief, really. Now at least I know where I'll be staying."

Chapter 6

Reverend Dean had called the police before they went to dinner, so a sheriff arrived shortly after Mary's confession. Leon accompanied the officer to the ferry, but Vicki seemed unable to move.

"This . . . this is all too much, Reverend."

"I know, my child. I'm sorry."

"But why, Reverend? Why would Mary kill those who had taken her in?"

"I think the answer was in her final words, Vicki. She'd been shuffled from one home to another while growing up, and when your father died she saw the same thing happening again. She knew that you and Leon wouldn't sell the estate, and since she couldn't bear to leave another home, she took matters into her own hands. I can't say it was rational, but it made sense to her."

"So Dad . . . *did* die naturally, then?"

"Yes. Mary was probably as distraught by your father's death as you were. He was the father, you were the sister, and your house was the home that she never felt she had. When he died everything crumbled, and she was prepared to do anything to preserve it."

"But what about the note Dad left. What about the curse?"

"There was no curse or ghost, Vicki. Mary wrote that note, and it was Mary who placed the muddy footprints from his hospital bed to the window. She had a moment of . . . 'evil inspiration,' shall we say, and she acted on it."

"But there's another thing, Reverend," Vicki said, looking at the pastor curiously. "We don't own a video cam, and I don't see how you could have fit an old one in your luggage. Where did you find one?"

"I never said I used a video cam, my child. I merely said that the ventilation grill would be an excellent place to locate one."

"But, the video cassette!"

The old man picked the VHS tape off the table. "Ah, you mean this one. It was fortunate she didn't call my bluff and look at the other side of this cassette. She would have seen that I'd borrowed it from your living room library."

Vicki's eye's widened. "Reverend! I can't believe it! What tape did you bring!?"

"I grabbed the closest tape, but when I saw the title it seemed coincidentally appropriate," the reverend smiled. He pushed the tape toward Vicki, who promptly turned it over.

Ghost Story.

"But then, *are* there really any coincidences in a Christian's life?" the old man asked, with a twinkle in his eye.

Murder from the Fourth Floor

Chapter 1

The two men — one young, one old — waited quietly on a sidewalk in front of a small Italian café in downtown Dark Pine. Although it was early September — the day after Labor Day, in fact — the morning was unusually cool. The old man glanced at his watch, then looked idly to his left. A bored meter maid, a jogger, and what looked like a businessman getting a head start on lunch were the only people in view.

To his right, the sidewalk was deserted. Cars lined the street. The curbside front tires of at least two autos appeared moist. Apparently a corner merchant had cleaned his sidewalk with a hose. Bored, the old man looked to the sky. It was clear and sunny. This disappointed him. He loved the rain, and it had been dry for almost a week. Far too long, in his judgment.

He smiled as he glanced at his young friend. Detective Mark Small was jingling the coins in his pants' pocket — a clear sign that he was impatient. Reverend Thaddeus Dean had known the thin man with gangly good-looks his entire life, and recognized every nuance of his behavior. He estimated that Mark would keep silent another fifteen seconds, then express his displeasure with the situation.

"I have no idea where Tim is," Mark blurted fourteen seconds later. "He knew we wanted to beat the noon rush, so he agreed to meet us at 11:30. It's 11:45. If he doesn't get here soon, we won't find a table."

"Why don't you use this time to explain why he wanted to meet us. If he isn't here in five minutes I'll go in and get a table, while you watch for him out here."

The twenty-six-year-old nodded in agreement, then collected his thoughts. "I've known Tim Dearborn since high school. He's a nurse at Dark Pine General. He's a smart guy, good at sports and popular with the ladies. Three years ago he married Betty Canaris. She's a VP at First National Bank."

"Actually, I know Betty," offered Reverend Dean. "She joined the church two years before I retired. She still attends regularly, but always alone."

"That sounds like Tim. He was never much for church. Anyway, it's Betty that he wants to talk about. They've recently separated, and Tim says that she's stalking him. He wants to talk it over with me and see what I can do. I told him that I was meeting you for lunch, and he said that was even better since you knew Betty."

"Why doesn't he just go to a lawyer?"

"He still hopes to reconcile, so he wants to keep things low-key. He figures that since I know her — and I'm a cop — she'll listen to me. At least, that's the pl—" Mark stopped, and abruptly peered over the reverend's squat frame. "There he is, at the corner."

The pastor followed Mark's gaze. A large man in his early

thirties — with brown hair, pleasant looks and a dark jacket — smiled and waved in their direction. He came within ten yards of the restaurant, then snapped his fingers as though he had forgotten something. Turning, he backtracked ten feet to a car he'd just passed. Mark didn't recognize the car, but he assumed it was Tim's. It was parked parallel to the sidewalk at the end of the block, five feet before the sidewalk ended and the cross-street began.

Tim stepped off the sidewalk and walked behind the car. As he did so, something seemed to catch his eye. He stopped in front of the trunk, shielded his eyes from the sun, and looked toward the top of an apartment building standing in the middle of the next block. Apparently intrigued by what he saw, he took a step toward the intersection.

That's when the shot rang out.

Tim grabbed his shoulder, spun around, and staggered several feet back to his car. Leaning against the trunk, he slumped quickly to the pavement.

As the wounded man sank from sight, Mark didn't hesitate; he immediately rushed to his stricken friend. He knew that Tim was a sitting duck for another shot. As Mark rounded the end of the car, he found his friend sitting against the bumper, grasping his arm. Knowing they might be in the cross-hairs of a rifle, Mark grabbed Tim by the lapels, pulled him to his knees, and immediately dragged him to the front of the car. With three thousand pounds of metal between them and the shooter, Mark looked back at the reverend. As expected, the old man had been smart enough to take shelter in the brick doorway of the restaurant.

"Call it in!" Mark yelled.

Satisfied that Mark was out of danger, and immensely proud of his bravery, the old man vanished inside the café.

Chapter 2

Five minutes later, Reverend Dean barely recognized the scene. Several police cars, an emergency medical van, and a tow truck occupied the street. Realizing that he couldn't help Mark, and concerned about Tim's injury, the old man struggled into the van and accompanied Tim Dearborn to the hospital.

Mark was glad to see the reverend leave harm's way. That allowed him to concentrate on the matter at hand — arresting the shooter, and avoid getting shot in the process.

Before the EMV arrived, Tim had told Mark that he'd seen movement at a window on the top floor of the apartment building. It typically wouldn't have caught his eye, except that Betty had leased the middle unit of that floor after they'd separated. He was positive the movement came from her window.

Even before the EMV left, Mark had positioned officers around the outside of the apartment, as well as indoors around the elevator and exits. Then he and two policemen ran up the stairs to the fourth floor, which was the top floor of the building.

However, instead of encountering a crazed shooter trying to escape, they encountered an elderly woman calmly knitting on a chair in the hallway.

"Ma'am, how long have you been sitting here?" Mark asked

urgently.

"Well," she replied, apparently unconcerned that men with guns had surrounded her, "that depends. What time is it?"

Mark was startled by her composure. "Well, it's uh . . . almost noon," he stammered.

"Then I've been sitting here almost two hours, young man. I come out every day at ten, when my husband turns on his professional wrestling show. Then I go in and fix his lunch at noon, when it's over." She glanced at his weapon. "I take it there's a problem?"

Mark almost smiled at the old woman. "Yes, ma'am," he said respectfully. "I'm afraid there is. Have you heard anything unusual this morning?"

"No," she replied, finally setting down her knitting. "But my husband sets the TV volume pretty high, and my hearing isn't what it used to be."

"Has anyone come out of an apartment while you've been sitting here today?"

"Not a soul."

"Do you know if any of these units are currently occupied?"

"I know the one next door is, because the door shut just as I was coming out to sit. That's Betty's apartment. The Jaxons live in the far rooms on that same side, but they're visiting relatives for the holiday. None of the three units on the other side of the hall are rented."

"Ma'am, thank you for your help. Now I have to ask you to get your husband and wait downstairs. It's important that you do so quickly and quietly."

As if expecting the request, Mrs. Dolly Bunion walked in her apartment, collected a baffled husband, and escorted him to the elevator. With the couple safely ensconced, Mark and his backup approached the middle unit. After each officer took position, Mark rapped on the door.

"To the person inside: this is the Dark Pine Police Department. Open your door immediately."

There was no response.

"Betty Dearborn! We know you're in there. This is the police. Open your door immediately!"

Silence. Thirty seconds later Mark turned to Patrolman Bosporus.

"Tom," he whispered, "break it down."

Tom Bosporus — fifty pounds heavier than anyone else on the force — stepped back, raised a booted foot, and slammed it against the door. One kick was all it took. The flimsy lock snapped and the door flew open. Greeting the officers with their drawn weapons was . . .

Nothing.

A quick search revealed that the apartment was empty. Mark approached the window, unlocked it, and cautiously peered outside. An officer on the ground looked up expectantly. Between them, lying on the fire escape outside the third floor, was a black teenager with an MP3 player and headphones. Mark could hear the rap music as soon as he opened the window. He turned to the officers behind him.

"I want every room on this floor searched. Then I want the other floors searched, including the roof. I'll finish this room and the fire exit."

After ensuring that the shooter wasn't hanging over the roof or peering out a window, Mark climbed slowly onto the fire escape. He was glad for an excuse to leave the room. In spite of the outside temperature, the sun had made the inside temperature uncomfortably warm. Worse, the smell of cordite from the gunpowder was overwhelming.

As soon as Mark stepped onto the fire escape, the vibration

from the railing caused the teenager to open his eyes. They opened wider when Mark's unbuttoned jacket revealed a gun and badge. The young man immediately removed his headphones. As he approached the teenager, Mark saw that he was at least eighteen years old. That would explain why he wasn't in school.

"I didn't mean to scare you. I'm Detective Mark Small, of the Dark Pine Police Department. I need to ask you a few questions."

"Uh, okay."

"How long have you been out here?"

"Since . . . I don't know, since about ten. As soon as the man upstairs started to watch his wrestling. He turns that TV up loud, you know? So I go out here and put on the 'phones. Drowns out the noise, you know?"

"So you came out here at ten?"

"As soon as the wrestling started. I din't look at no clock."

"Did anyone come up or down the fire escape while you were here?"

"No, man. I woulda seen 'em."

"You didn't fall asleep out here?"

"No, man. I was jus' chillen' 'til the old man turned his set off."

"Did you hear anything while you were out here?"

The teenager looked at Mark as though he was crazy. Then Mark recalled the headphone volume.

"Uh . . . right. Never mind. Look, did you notice anything out of the ordinary this morning? There was a shooting on the street below."

"Uh-uh. Not me. It came from here?"

"Maybe. Anyway, someone will be up in a few minutes to take your statement. Here's my card. If you remember anything, give me a call, okay?"

Mark climbed back in the room and began a more thorough search. A shell casing lay about three feet to the right of the window, exactly where it would fall if a rifle had been fired from that spot. He was surprised by the caliber, however. A .22. Professional assassins sometimes used that caliber in handguns for close-up hits. It was powerful enough to penetrate the skull, but didn't retain enough energy to exit the cranium. Consequently, it ricocheted around the brain and did an ugly amount of damage. A .22 *rifle*, however, was a boy's gun.

Or maybe . . . a woman's.

But there was a bigger question. Where was Betty Dearborn? Clearly this was the unit where the shot came from. The odor and brass confirmed that. Moreover, the old lady saw Betty — Mark corrected himself, saw *someone* — enter the apartment at 10:00. But neither the lady in the hallway, nor the teenager on the fire escape, saw anyone *leave* the apartment.

Mark searched the ceiling for crawl spaces, and the floor for trap doors. There were none. He checked the walls for any access to adjacent apartments. They were all solid. He looked under the bed, in the closet, behind the shower curtain, and under the sink. After fifteen minutes, he would stake his badge that there were no hidden exits or hiding places in Betty Dearborn's apartment.

So how did the woman get out?

Chapter 3

The medical van jerked to a stop in front of the ER entrance. With brisk efficiency the med techs wheeled Tim Dearborn through a set of automatic doors and into an examination room. Knowing that was a restricted area, Reverend Dean shuffled to a brightly colored chair in a nearby waiting room. During his years as pastor of Dark Pine Community Church, the old man had been to D.P. General more times than he could count. It was part of a reverend's calling; to comfort those in the hospital, as well as their friends and loved ones.

But he had never gotten used to it.

After quietly sitting in the chair, the cleric unobtrusively bowed his head, and silently prayed for the man he'd just met in the bowels of an emergency van.

Thirty minutes later, a young doctor emerged from the exam room and approached the reverend. "Are you waiting for Tim Dearborn?"

"Yes," replied the reverend.

"He'll be fine. He's dressing now. You can go and see him if you'd like."

"Thank you, doctor."

Reverend Dean struggled up from the chair and walked to the

room indicated by the doctor. The old man shook his head. He was amazed at how young physicians looked nowadays. He remembered when they seemed so much older than he was.

"Hello, Reverend. You didn't have to wait for me."

Reverend Dean's newest friend was wearing an undershirt and pants, and was pulling on a sock when the cleric entered. For the first time — his view was obstructed in the van — he was able to get a close look at Tim. The retiree approved. Although Tim's face had fewer wrinkles than most, he'd developed the type of crow's feet that were usually caused by frequent smiling and laughter.

"It was no trouble, Tim. What's the prognosis?"

"I was pretty lucky," he said gratefully. "The bullet passed through my arm and completely missed the bone. They say I should be as good as new in a few weeks."

"That's wonderful news, Tim! I'm very happy for you."

"I'm happy, too," he began, "but I can't believe—" Tim stopped, and struggled to suppress some internal emotion. "Did Mark tell you that . . . that it was *Betty* who shot me?"

The reverend was stunned. "No! We haven't spoken. Tim, are you *sure*?"

"As sure as I can be. I didn't actually see her, but I saw a reflection, then something stick out her apartment window, and then . . . bam! You saw the rest."

"Betty *lives* in those apartments?"

"Sure. That's what I wanted to talk to you about. Didn't Mark mention that?"

"Somewhat. He mentioned that you and Betty had separated, and I assumed that one of you had moved out. But I didn't know she lived in those apartments."

Tim glanced ruefully at his arm. "She's doing a lot of things that no one knew about."

The young man struggled to slip his feet into a pair of worn penny loafers. After sliding them on he kept his head bowed, staring at the floor. He'd maintained a strong façade so far, but slowly his demeanor began to crack. It looked as if he was going to cry.

"Reverend . . . I know you've counseled a lot of couples, and that's the main reason I wanted to see you. I *love* Betty. She's . . . she's the one who *completes* me, Reverend. Do you know what I mean?"

Reverend Dean nodded. He knew.

"But . . . what do you do when the most important person in the world — the person who knows you better than anyone else — decides that you don't deserve to live? Reverend, how do I *deal* with that?"

Reverend Dean offered a silent prayer for guidance, then attempted to answer an almost unanswerable question. "Tim . . . it's important to remember that no one knows us completely except God. Betty's actions can't diminish the fact that you're made in His image, and therefore of inestimable value. Don't let the opinion of Betty, or anyone else, detract from that truth."

Tim considered those comments as he shrugged on his shirt. The injured man moved so slowly that it was painful to watch him dress.

"I . . . I hope you're right."

"I am, my son. You are so important that God died on your behalf. You are, literally, of eternal worth."

Tim nodded. The reverend couldn't tell if he agreed or not. His heart ached for the young man.

"Will you talk to her, Reverend? Will you tell her what you've told me? I'd do anything to get her back."

"Of course, Tim. It would be my privilege."

A cumbersome silence followed. Eventually, Tim asked a more direct question.

"What happened after we left, Reverend? Did Mark go into the building after Betty?"

The reverend nodded at the door as Tim finished his question. "Why don't you ask *him* that," he suggested.

"Hello, Tim," Mark said, entering the room. "How's the arm?"

"I was just telling the reverend that it'll be fine. But what happened after I left? Did you arrest Betty?"

The detective's smile vanished. Knowing Mark as he did, the reverend cocked an eyebrow. Something was wrong.

"We . . . didn't find her," Mark began. "But we will. You have my word on that."

Tim finished buttoning his shirt and looked miserably at Mark. "Just don't . . . *hurt* her, okay?" he pleaded. "Can you give me your word on *that*?"

"We'll discuss that and much more, my friend, while I drive you home."

Tim looked startled. "What about my car?"

"Tim, you can't drive with one arm. I'd have to arrest you and that would embarrass both of us," Mark teased. "But even if you could, the bullet grazed the fender of your car. We had to impound it as part of the crime scene."

"What? For how long?"

Mark held up both hands in appeasement. "Not long. Forty-eight hours, seventy-two tops. Besides, it's not like you could drive it during that time, right?"

"Well . . . I suppose. Now that you mention it, I'll probably have trouble making dinner, too. You're forgiven if you stop by McDonald's on the way home."

"Done," grinned Mark, as they exited the room.

Behind Tim's back, Mark glanced at Reverend Dean. His smile abruptly vanished, and the old man saw that he was troubled. "Reverend, I'll call *you* tonight."

Chapter 4

Reverend Dean left the hospital and walked to his dilapidated Ford. The car was even older than Puppadawg, his elderly St. Bernard. However, instead of driving home, he stopped by the local grocery store to do a little shopping.

Although he wasn't exactly poor, Reverend Dean had never accumulated much money. So over time he had found various ways to economize. Today, for example, there would be a good selection of three-day-old bread on sale. If he was lucky, there would also be hamburger in the meat section with that day's expiration date. That was usually good for thirty percent off.

But he considered himself particularly fortunate if there were bags of ripe bananas in the fruit department. Those small sacks were usually no more than twenty-five cents each. More importantly, however, that meant he could make his favorite desert, banana pudding — if he splurged and bought vanilla wafers and pudding mix.

Which he invariably did.

The only remaining item on his list was a bag of dog food for Puppadawg. The monstrous St. Bernard required the largest bag in the store, but that didn't bother Reverend Dean. He rationalized that, pound for pound, it was also the most economical.

Unfortunately, the bag was too bulky for the old man to lift. He solved half that problem by asking a stock boy to carry it to his car. When he arrived home, he retrieved a wheelbarrow from the garage, pushed it to his Ford, and slowly pulled the huge bag from the trunk into the tray. This was always difficult for the reverend, but as soon as he heard the enormous hound bellow his greeting, all inconvenience was forgotten.

After a quick word with Puppadawg, Reverend Dean put the hamburger and bread in the refrigerator, and set to work on his pudding.

Mark arrived five hours later. Their relationship was more like father-son than friend-friend, so the detective gave a cursory knock and walked in without waiting for an answer. He found the old man taking a large glass bowl out of the refrigerator. He immediately knew what it was.

"Bananas on sale today?" he teased kindly.

"I can eat it by myself, if you're not interested," the reverend joked. They both knew that Mark loved banana pudding as much as the reverend.

"Well, I wouldn't want you to eat *alone*," Mark smiled, reaching for a bowl in the cabinet. "You know, I think I'd actually marry Debbie if she learned how to make banana pudding like you do. The one time she tried, it was hot and runny. I've never encouraged her since. Can I send her over for lessons?"

"Of course. I'm sure she'd handle the suggestion that an old man cooks better than she does with perfect aplomb."

"Uh, well . . . there is that. Maybe you could teach me, and she could watch while *I* made it."

"Mark, have you ever made *anything* other than TV dinners?"

"I could *learn*," Mark retorted, with mock seriousness.

"No doubt. But it would be less taxing if you simply married this longsuffering woman, and visited me whenever bananas were on sale."

"*Longsuffering?*"

The old man merely smiled, with a twinkle in his eye.

"Okay," replied Mark, "if you won't discuss that, let's try another topic. Betty and Tim Dearborn. How are you at solving vanishings?"

"I can listen," the cleric replied, with more interest than he let on.

Mark described the raid in detail. Reverend Dean, as good as his word, listened attentively. By the time Mark was finished, the cleric had several questions.

"So the three reasons you think Betty was in that apartment are the smell of gunpowder, the shell casing, and the allegation of a neighbor that she saw the door close."

"Well, keep in mind the neighbor watched Betty's door until we arrived. But there's more. Betty called her mother while she was inside."

"What? When?" The reverend was surprised.

"An hour after the neighbor saw her door close. At 11:05."

"How do you know this?"

"Betty's mother lives in Spokane. The call was long-distance, so it came up when we checked her phone log."

"Have you talked with the mother?"

"Only by phone. Betty didn't actually speak with her. She called Spokane, listened to the recording on her mom's machine, and waited for her mother to answer. When she didn't, she hung up."

Reverend Dean considered this for several seconds.

"Any other reasons to think she was present?"

"Yes. We interviewed everyone else in the apartment complex. Every single tenant has an alibi. Either they weren't home, or they were inside with multiple witnesses."

"Are there any vacant units on the side of the building facing the café?"

"All units on that side of the complex are rented, except for one on the second floor. We checked those rooms thoroughly, and no one's been in them for weeks. But the first three floors don't matter, because we found the slug embedded in the street under Tim's car. The angle of the bullet matches the top floor of the apartment building. It couldn't have come from any other floor."

Mark stopped the reverend before he could ask his next question.

"And, in case you're wondering, the bullet we recovered was definitely the bullet that hit Tim. It had traces of chrome from his bumper, traces of fiber from his coat, and traces of blood. It'll take awhile before we get DNA confirmation that it's Tim's blood, but we've already determined that it's O negative, which is Tim's type."

The reverend leaned forward, scratched what little of his hair remained, and rested a pudgy elbow on the table. "Mark, I know Betty. I simply can't believe she'd do something like this."

"I know her too, Reverend. And before today, I'd agree. But I can't ignore the evidence."

Reverend Dean nodded absent-mindedly. Surely there was *something* that could explain Betty's actions. "Mark, please describe the fourth floor to me."

"There's nothing unusual," he shrugged. "It's an older apartment building, with six units on every floor, including the fourth floor, which is the top level. Three units have windows facing the crime scene, while the remaining three units sit across the hall, with windows overlooking the opposite side of the building."

He knew that Mark thought this was unnecessary, but he persisted. "Go on. What's the interior like?"

Mark sighed, then continued. "The hallway is hardwood, covered by one of those long, narrow, oriental carpets . . . what do you call them?"

"Runners."

"Exactly. It begins a few feet before you reach Betty's door, and extends to the end of the hallway. It's wide enough so that it almost touches the walls on either side of the hall."

Mark paused, then moved to the unit itself. "The apartments have identical floor plans, with one bedroom, one bath, a den and a small kitchen. The main window in each apartment opens onto an exterior fire escape. A much smaller window, which has glass louvers that crank open with a handle, is in the bedroom. The louvers can't be removed, so no one can climb in or out of that window. As you've probably guessed, the building is pretty old. It was probably built in the 1940s.

"What was the condition of the apartment?"

Mark glanced at the ceiling and visualized the layout. "Nothing unusual. It's a small apartment, so it was fairly cluttered. As you enter, there's a small table by the door. It had a tray to hold outgoing letters, a picture of Betty's mother, yesterday's newspaper, some junk mail, a box to keep keys in, and a phone. In fact, I almost tripped over the cord when I entered the apartment."

"Were there any outgoing letters in the tray?"

"No."

"Any keys in the box?"

"No."

"Go on."

"The living room had a sofa, a chair and a coffee table in between them. There was a remote for the TV on the table, and a phone book underneath. The kitchen was clean and well stocked. In her bedroom, the bed had been made, and all her clothes were either hung up or folded in a small dresser in a corner of the room.

"Anything on top of the dresser?"

Mark furrowed. "Not that I recall."

"What was the bathroom like?"

"Neatly arranged. A razor and bottle of shampoo in the shower. Typical items in the cabinet behind the mirror and in the drawers. Nothing else."

Mark was right. Nothing seemed unusual about the building or the apartment. "You said the other tenants had alibis. How about reversing the query. Were any of them witnesses?"

"Good question, but no. No one saw anything that morning. But. . ."

"Yes?"

"Someone on the first floor did see something weird, if you can believe him. He strikes me as an early-twenties slacker. I wouldn't be surprised if he was high on something when he looked out his window, but. . ."

"What did he see?"

"He says he saw a yellow snake slither past his window."

"A yellow *snake*?"

Mark nodded. "But, as you know, there are no yellow snakes in Washington. I doubt there are any in the *country*. But even if there were, it's irrelevant. The shooting was the next morning, and this happened at 11:30 the preceding night."

"Was he alone?"

"No. He was with his girlfriend."

"Did she confirm this . . . sighting?"

Mark screwed up his face; a common reaction when he was confronted with inconvenient facts. "In a way. In fact, that's the only reason I mention it, because she saw something, too. But she didn't think it was a snake. She says it looked like a rope."

"Was it yellow?"

"She's not sure. She only got a glimpse of it."

"Well they must have seen *something*."

"Perhaps. But I can't see how it has anything to do with Betty."

Reverend Dean wasn't so sure, but it was difficult to tie a yellow snake to an attempted murder. He mentally filed this strange account for further review. "Were there witnesses to anything else?"

"No, although tenants heard various noises throughout the night. There was an argument in an upstairs apartment, loud music in a downstairs apartment, people running up the stairs, people running down the stairs, inside doors slamming, outside doors slamming, a car's backfire, a police siren . . . you name it. And, of course, any number of alarms. A smoke alarm, a car alarm, even an alarm for keeping the elevator door open. In other words," he sighed, "the usual sounds in a downtown apartment."

Reverend Dean was forced to agree. This analysis had gotten them nowhere. "So what's the next step?" he finally inquired. "How do you plan to find Betty?"

"There are only so many places she can hide in Dark Pine. We have an APB on her car, and we're watching Sea-Tac as well as the bus stations. But I'm guessing she's still in town. We'll find her — sooner, rather than later, I think."

"Will you be able to capture her peaceably?"

"That depends on Betty, but I hope so. Then she can answer the question of the day — how did she get out of a sealed apartment without anyone seeing her?"

Chapter 5

Reverend Dean's phone rang at precisely 10:00 the following morning. He deduced several things from this fact. Number one, it was someone who knew him. All of his friends knew he was an incorrigible night owl, and that he stayed up until 2:00 every morning. As a result, he always slept until 10:00 AM. Consequently, this was no stranger.

Number two, the call was important — at least to the caller — because he (or she) didn't call at 10:30, or even 10:15; but at exactly 10:00.

The reverend revised his deduction as he sat up in bed. Rather than an important call, perhaps the caller was merely impatient. Or an impatient caller with important information. Regardless, he knew only one person who fit all these criteria, and smiled as he picked up the receiver.

"Hello, Mark," he yawned.

"Hel—. Hey, how did you know it was me?"

"An old man needs a few secrets, my son. What's happened?"

"Why do you think. . ." Mark paused, then took a calming breath. "You're right, Reverend. Something *has* happened. We found Betty this morning. She's . . . Reverend, she's committed suicide."

Reverend Dean bolted straight up, eyes wide open. "Oh no, Mark. Oh no, no."

"I'm sorry, Reverend. I know she was close to you."

"Oh, Mark. . ." The reverend's face sank in his hands. Such a beautiful, talented girl. Now she was gone forever. "Mark, are . . . you sure it was suicide?"

"Yes. In fact, we've just finished here." Mark didn't elaborate. The reverend assumed that others were listening, and that Mark couldn't say anything more. "I have to break the news to Tim. Would you like to meet at Starbucks later on? Say, at 1:00?"

"I'll be there."

Reverend Dean was devastated. In spite of what she'd done, Betty was a wonderful girl. Even if she went to jail for shooting Tim, she would still have enjoyed a long life afterward. It was such a senseless tragedy.

The old man pulled on his clothes, walked to his backyard and called for Puppadawg. The enormous beast galloped to its master. Thaddeus Dean hugged his pet, fell to the ground, and cried.

Reverend Dean walked into the world's smallest Starbucks far sooner than Mark had suggested. He told himself that he was just in the mood for coffee. But that wasn't true. He just didn't want to be alone.

The coffee shop was little more than a kiosk, with six comfortable chairs and a smattering of palm fronds. Even at this size he was amazed that Dark Pine warranted such a franchise. But he counted his blessings every time he tasted a Grande Latte.

Until today. Today it tasted bland. Just like his breakfast. Just like he felt.

In such a small environment Mark had no trouble finding his elderly friend. The detective purchased his own latte, shook chemicals into it, stirred the brew with a wooden wand too short and narrow for the task, and sat across from the reverend.

"Hello, Mark."

"Reverend."

They sat in silence for several seconds. Eventually, the old man spoke. "How did Tim take it?"

Mark shrugged. He didn't want to dwell on it. "He broke down."

Reverend Dean nodded. As much as anyone, he knew what it was like to lose a spouse. "Mark, tell me where — and how — they found her."

The detective carefully set his latte in the middle of a small napkin. "Betty was found in her car with the same rifle she used to shoot Tim. We've matched the bullets. She printed a suicide note, drove to the park near I-90, and shot herself through the eye."

The reverend had been staring at his drink until Mark's final word. "Through the *eye*?"

Mark nodded.

"What did the note say?"

"It's against regulations, but I thought you'd like to see it, since you knew Betty." Dark Pine's junior detective cautiously pulled a sheet of paper — sealed in a plastic bag — out of his pocket and slid it toward the reverend. He placed his forearms on either side of the table to shield the evidence from prying eyes.

"Mark, this is . . . *typed*."

"Well, word-processed and printed, but you're right."

The reverend read the note.

Divorce is bad enough, but losing a career,
going to jail, and emerging destitute is too much.
I'm sorry for everything.
Betty

The old man pushed the note gently across the table. "Thank you for letting me see it."

To Mark's surprise, a gleam appeared in the reverend's eyes. Although the sadness lingered, he seemed less despondent. Almost . . . energized.

"What's going on, Reverend?" Mark asked, squinting at the old man. "I know you. If your mind worked any harder, there'd be smoke coming out your ears."

"Mark," the pastor began slowly, "you realize this wasn't a suicide."

Mark exhaled loudly and looked out the window in annoyance. "I *knew* I shouldn't have let you see that letter."

The reverend was unimpressed. "*You* know it too. That's *why* you let me see it. You wanted confirmation."

"Really? Okay, enlighten me. Why isn't Betty's death a suicide?"

"I'm not telling you anything you don't already know, but I'll share the reasons anyway." The reverend held up a stubby finger. "One, she's a woman who used a gun to supposedly commit suicide. Most women don't use that method."

"True. But forty percent do. That's no proof."

The reverend extended a second finger. "Two, she shot herself through the eye. Almost no one, male *or* female, does that. They aim at the chest, head or mouth."

Mark sighed. "I'll give you that. But it's not enough."

Reverend Dean raised a third finger. "She used a *rifle* to shoot herself in a *car*. That's incredibly awkward. And unusual."

"Awkward, I grant you. But so what? Maybe a rifle was the only firearm she owned. Given her behavior, I *hope* it was."

"Four," the reverend continued, "why would she type a suicide note on a word processor? Aren't most suicide notes handwritten?"

"Most," Mark conceded. "But not all."

The reverend stuck out his thumb. "Finally, consider her kitchen. When you described it to me, you said it was well-stocked. Would someone who was contemplating suicide fill her pantry before she killed herself?"

"Perhaps . . . uh, perhaps not. But it's not like most suicides are *rational*, Reverend."

"Betty was."

"Does a rational person shoot someone else?"

Reverend Dean gripped his warm paper cup and drained the latte. "Not usually," he admitted, as he set the container down. "Which means we're missing something. And we have to find it."

Chapter 6

The old man waved goodbye as Mark drove back to work. As he stood on the sidewalk, noting the sunny sky with displeasure, he was convinced that Betty's death was no suicide.

But how could he prove it?

He was confident that Mark would check Betty's hands for gunpowder residue. If present, it supported the theory that she shot herself. Unless, of course, the particles were remnants from her attempt on Tim's life. The reverend shook his head. There were so many variables. He needed to clear his head and let his subconscious ponder the matter.

The best way to clear his mind was usually to browse the local bookstore. Dark Pine had only one such business, a locally-owned store near Starbucks. Although it was small, the staff was friendly, and the log fireplace and overstuffed chairs were irresistible. Given the circumstances, however, he knew he wouldn't be able to concentrate. Instead, he slowly shuffled to his car.

Fifteen minutes later, he opened the door to Betty Dearborn's apartment building.

Although there was a small lobby at the entrance — a rarity in modern apartments, but common in older buildings — he couldn't discern a manager's office. Undeterred, he walked to the elevator, stepped inside and poked the fourth floor button. As the machine jerked and creaked to its destination, he wondered if he should have taken the stairs. Eventually, however, the weary elevator deposited him on the top floor.

He was abruptly met by an elderly woman reading a book in the hallway.

"You'd be interested in Betty, I suppose," the lady declared, eyes never leaving her book. The tone of her voice belied her thin, frail appearance.

Surprised by her acumen as well as her demeanor, the reverend was less than eloquent. "Er . . . yes, actually."

The woman nodded in satisfaction, set the book on the lap of her dress, and examined her visitor. "Why?"

The reverend had to grin. "Why *not?*" he rejoined.

After a pause, the old woman smiled back, apparently satisfied with the reverend's response. "Dolly Bunion," she stated, holding out her hand.

"Thaddeus Dean," he replied, impressed with the woman's grip as well as her attire. Although it was doubtful she expected visitors, the aged Mrs. Bunion still dressed for the occasion, even though she had merely gone to the hallway to read a book. Reverend Dean lamented the fact that only his generation did that anymore. If this esteemed lady had been forty years younger, she would doubtless have worn sweatpants and tennis shoes.

"She went to your church?" inquired Dolly.

"Mrs. Bunion, I have to say I'm impressed with your deductions."

"Don't be. The Jaxons and I have lived here for years. I know their friends, and you're not one of them. So you must be here about Betty. And I know you're a pastor because my husband and I visited your church a decade ago."

"Since you never returned, I must have delivered an uninspiring sermon."

"Actually, it held my interest — which is more than I can say for most sermons. But we only came because my husband's niece was visiting, and she wanted to go to a church. We picked yours because it was closest. No offense."

"None taken, Mrs. Bunion."

"Dolly."

"Thank you, Dolly."

"I expect you know that Betty isn't home. Which means you want to examine the premises, talk to me, or both. I like Betty. I want to help her. What can I tell you?"

What a unique woman. Reverend Dean was delighted to meet her. Unfortunately, the admirable Mrs. Bunion added little to what she'd told Mark. Now that he'd met her, he wasn't surprised. Dolly's mind was sharp, and she'd relayed everything she knew to the police. There was simply nothing left to tell. Realizing this, he changed subjects.

"Dolly, thank you for repeating what you saw. I believe that's all I need to know. Do you think it would be alright if I examined Betty's door?"

The old woman shrugged. "I won't tell."

He smiled and walked to the locked apartment. The hallway was exactly as Mark described. An oriental runner, wider than most, extended almost to the walls on either side. Surprisingly, the frame around the door had already been repaired from the police break-in. The door itself was solid — not hollow, like most modern doors — and appeared unaltered except for the addition of a deadbolt lock. Unlike most entry doors, however, there was no weatherboard to seal the area between the bottom of the door and the floor. Presumably that was because it was, technically, an interior door. He shrugged. Perhaps that accounted for the slight breeze he felt around his ankles. Acting on an impulse he reached down and inserted his fingers under the door.

There was no breeze, which made sense. Mark would never allow the window of a crime scene to remain open.

Pivoting, he knelt and stuck his fingers beneath the door across the hall. Ah. That was the source. But no one lived in that apartment. Why would a window be open? He turned to his newfound friend. "Dolly, do you know why a window would be open in this apartment?"

Dolly had returned to her book. "Nope," she replied, with her usual brevity.

He scanned the hallway once more, then returned to the august Mrs. Bunion and offered his hand.

"Dolly, I have thoroughly enjoyed meeting you. Although I've retired as pastor, I would love to sit with you and your husband at church, should you ever feel inclined to visit."

Dolly accepted his hand. "We'll see, Pastor. Stranger things have happened." The old woman looked down the hall at Betty's apartment. "Yes, sir, stranger things have happened indeed."

After walking downstairs — he decided not to test the elevator again — Reverend Dean stood outside the main entrance to the apartment and looked at the sky. It hadn't rained in over a week, and to him that was tantamount to a drought. Fortunately, it looked as if this plague was near an end. Dark clouds were forming to the west, and the Weather Channel — which he watched devotedly — promised a downpour this evening.

The portly cleric was waddling to his car when he noticed a mother and daughter leaving a nearby restaurant. The mother had licked a napkin and was using it to wipe a scuff mark off her daughter's shoe. Midway through the task, the woman's cell phone rang and the parent abandoned her chore in lieu of taking the call. Twenty seconds later, her small patience exhausted, the girl tugged on her mother's sleeve. Unmoved, the woman spent another minute on the phone, snapped it shut, finished cleaning the shoe and whisked her daughter into an SUV.

All in all, it was difficult to imagine a more mundane exchange between two people. And yet. . .

And yet it made him think of something. He cocked his head, and a gleam appeared in his eyes.

He had some important questions for Mark.

He didn't want to use a public phone, and he'd never owned a cell, so he drove home as fast as the speed limit allowed. He couldn't remember the last time he'd driven this fast, and was pleasantly surprised that his aged Ford could achieve it.

The cleric pulled in his driveway, ignored Puppadawg's greeting, and phoned Mark.

"Detective Small."

"Mark, this is . . . this is . . . well you *know* who this is," blurted Reverend Dean. "I think I know how Betty left her apartment."

Mark didn't know whether to be amused at the reverend's enthusiasm or pleased at the prospect of a breakthrough. He opted for the latter.

"Great. How?"

"First I need to ask four questions."

Mark's interest abruptly waned. Apparently the reverend hadn't solved anything after all. "Reverend, you already know everything I do about this case."

"Then be kind and refresh an old man's memory."

"Oh . . . very well. Shoot."

"How big was the table next to Betty's front door?"

"Uh, Reverend, are you sure this is a productive use of—"

"*Yes*, Mark," the cleric replied, in his most authoritative voice. He only used this tone when a request was important, and it never failed to get results. This time was no exception.

"It was maybe . . . maybe nine inches by eighteen inches. A skinny rectangle."

"Thank you. Was the door stop screwed into the wall, or into the door?"

"The door stop? You mean . . . the short rod that keeps a door from slamming into the wall? Judas, Reverend, I have no idea. I'd have to pull the photos of the apartment."

"Will you do that and bring them over tonight?"

Mark sighed. "I'd *planned* to go out with *Debbie* tonight. Anything *else*?"

The reverend had to smile. But whether Mark knew it or not, this was important.

"Yes. You said that Betty phoned her mother when she was in her apartment. Did you press the redial button to see if she called anyone after that?"

"Actually, I did. It didn't work. In fact, the phone beeped at me."

"It . . . *beeped* at you?"

"Yes. And your last question?"

"Has the lab finished its exam of Tim's car?"

"Yes. They found nothing beyond the bullet damage."

"Nothing?"

"*Nothing*, Reverend. Are you through?"

"For now," he replied cryptically.

Chapter 7

Detective Mark Small parked behind Reverend Dean's Ford, rapped once on the door, and walked into the old man's house. The reverend was standing in the living room, his back to the door, staring out the window.

"Deep thoughts?" the detective asked.

The old man didn't move. "I suppose. I was wondering how someone could snuff out a young life in full bloom, merely to solve his or her own problems."

"I'm the wrong person to ask, Reverend. You're the theologian."

The reverend nodded without responding. Finally he turned and faced his young friend. "I've been doing some other thinking as well. You've brought the photos, I trust?"

Mark tossed a large manila folder onto the coffee table. "Here they are. But I can save you the trouble. Betty's door stop—"

"—was screwed into the door, rather than the wall."

"Well, yes. How did you know?"

"It's the only way it could have happened."

"The only way *what* could have happened, Reverend?"

"How Betty disappeared."

"So you've been saying. I still haven't heard your theory."

Reverend Dean patted Mark on the shoulder, smiled sadly, and walked to the head of the stairs. "It's a little chilly, so I made a fire downstairs. I've also filled two bowls with banana pudding. I hope you don't object?"

"Lead on."

After stoking the fire and handing Mark his pudding, Reverend Dean sank into a well-worn recliner. The fragrant smell of burning logs wafted through the den. "Here's what I believe happened. I need to tell it in chronological order, so I'll start before Tim was shot."

Mark's mouth was full of banana pudding, so he simply grunted.

"I'll take that as a 'yes,'" the reverend replied, with a twinkle in his eye, "and make a note that I've failed to discuss certain social graces with you."

Mark smiled as he shoveled another spoon of pudding into his mouth.

"I'm not going to tell you who I think the shooter was, because I don't think you'd believe me. Instead I'll describe how he — or she — *left* the apartment."

Mark swallowed and spoke up.

"Reverend, you don't have to tell me who it was. It's not like it could be anyone except Betty."

"Really? How about Dolly?"

"Who?"

"The elderly neighbor who sat in the hallway. You spoke with her. So did I, this afternoon."

"Mrs. Bunion?"

"She has no one to confirm her statement. For that matter, neither does Mr. Bunion. You've spoken to him, I assume? He was out when I visited."

Mark hesitated. "Ah . . . not yet," he confessed.

"We also have the gentleman on the fire escape. Mr. . ."

"Demming. Juwan Demming."

"Have you checked his story? Did he know Betty? Or Tim?"

"We, uh . . . haven't finished checking that out yet." Mark laid his empty bowl on the scuffed end table. He was embarrassed.

Reverend Dean quickly sought to reassure the young man. "All I'm saying is that we have to reexamine our assumptions in order to solve this case."

"All right, fine. So what do you think happened?"

"Betty was never in her apartment. But the shooter was."

Intrigued, Mark leaned forward. He may have made too many assumptions, but he rarely made the same mistake twice. "Someone other than Betty? When?"

"Sometime before 10:00 AM."

The detective immediately objected. "Reverend, we examined her door. It hadn't been forced."

"That's true. The intruder used Betty's key."

"What, she just *gave* it away?"

Reverend Dean paused, then looked at his fingernails. "I rather think it was . . . taken from her," he said quietly. "You see, she'd already been kidnapped by that point."

"She'd been . . . *what!*?"

"Sit back and I'll try to explain. It might go more quickly if you hold your questions for a bit."

Mark's expression implied that the reverend had gone senile. Still, he respected the old man enough to hear him out.

"I don't know how the shooter arranged the kidnapping and — to be honest — I don't want to contemplate it. In any event, once the intruder entered the apartment, he or she dropped a spent shell casing near the window. That accounts for the brass you found. The shooter then emptied a packet of loose gunpowder into a bowl; perhaps from Betty's own kitchen. A match was put to the powder, which promptly burned. That accounts for the smell of cordite in the unit. It also explains why — even when the apartment was quite warm — the window was closed. The shooter didn't want the smell to dissipate. He or she *wanted* you to smell it."

"But the door closing, the phone call, the—"

Reverend Dean raised a hand and tilted his head. "Patience, patience," he replied soothingly. "Let me ask you a question, Mark. When you originally described Betty's apartment, you said that it was 'cluttered.' And your description of the entryway table certainly suggested that. But when you described her living room, bedroom and bathroom, it didn't sound cluttered at all. In fact, Betty had nothing on her dresser, nothing on her bathroom counter, and just a TV remote on her living room table. Doesn't that strike you as odd?"

"Maybe she was one of those people who dumped everything on the first surface she saw. In her case, it was the entryway table."

Reverend Dean shook his head. "I don't think so. Don't you remember how you almost tripped over the phone cord when you entered her apartment? I suggest that no one puts a phone in a spot where they might trip over its cord every time they come through the door."

"That . . . *is* unusual," Mark admitted. "So why was it there?"

Reverend Dean paused and looked down at his feet. He was getting too old for this, he reflected. There was so much evil in the world. Too much. It seemed impossible to bear. Then he reminded himself that he didn't have to solve everything; just what God assigned him. He took a deep breath, and continued.

"The phone was there because the shooter *moved* it there. Do you recall the phone book under the coffee table in the living room? I believe the phone usually rested on top of *that* table, next to the TV remote. It would be far more practical."

"Okay, but why move it?"

"Do you remember when I asked if you'd pushed the redial button on Betty's handset?"

"Yes. It didn't work."

"Actually, you said it *beeped* at you. Would you like to know one explanation for that?"

Mark was out of his league, but fortunately had the sense to know it. He quietly nodded.

"One explanation is that it was out of range of its receiver."

"Reverend, it was *on* its receiver."

"No, my son. It was on *a* receiver. All the shooter needed to do was buy an identical cordless phone, then place the new handset on Betty's old receiver. In order for the old receiver to continue to work, the new handset just needed to sit slightly askew in the cradle, so that the prongs of the handset didn't touch the plates of the receiver. More importantly, once Betty's old receiver was moved to the entryway table, it would be close enough for the intruder to use Betty's original handset from the apartment across the hall. *That's* why Betty's old receiver was moved. The shooter took her original handset, entered the vacant unit by breaking a window, and — after Dolly took her 10:00 vigil in the hallway — called Betty's mother in Spokane. Later, when you entered Betty's unit, it appeared that Betty's real handset was in her apartment, resting on its receiver."

"Ah ha! So it wasn't Mrs. Bunion."

The old man smiled. "You're right. Dolly was telling the truth."

"Well, that . . . *could* work," Mark frowned, "but why do something that's so easily checked?"

"Because it didn't have to fool anyone for long. For all we know, the shooter has already replaced the original handset on the receiver."

Mark was impressed. He'd never heard of such a scheme, but

there was no reason it couldn't work. And his men *had* noticed a small break in the vacant unit's window. In their hunt for the hidden shooter, however, they hadn't thought it important.

Then he held up a cautionary finger. "But you're forgetting that Mrs. Bunion saw Betty close her door."

"Actually, she saw *someone* close the door. And here's how it was done. Do you remember my question about the door stop?"

Mark grunted. "How could I forget? It was unusual, even for you."

The reverend smiled, then held up both hands. "If someone had a long piece of, let's say, fishing line leader — you know, the line that's strong and clear, so fish can't see that it's attached to a hook — and fed it under the runner in the hallway, it would be impossible to see."

"Well, I suppose. . ."

"If he then looped — not tied — that line around the door stop attached to Betty's door, and hid in the apartment across the hall, he could tug on both ends of the leader, which would pull the door shut. After that, he could simply pull one end of the line back into the unit he was hiding in — under the hallway rug — and no one would notice it."

"But that's taking a big risk. What if the neighbor saw that no one was standing in Betty's unit when the door was shut?"

"Actually, it wasn't risky at all. The runner started several feet from Betty's door. If Dolly approached Betty's unit, the shooter would hear her footsteps on the hardwood floor. Once her shoes hit the runner, he'd pull the line. As it turned out, however, he simply shut the door as soon as Dolly came out of her apartment to knit."

Mark threw up his hands in frustration.

"But why go to all this *trouble*? What was the *point*?"

"Mark, what have we done for most of this case? We've

obsessed over how Betty escaped from her room. The shooter did this to focus us on *how* she escaped, so that we'd spend less time on *who* did it, and *why*. And — until now — it's worked," he admitted.

"Reverend, this is too much. I admit this might be — *might* be — possible. But you're avoiding the main problem, which is this: Tim was *shot*. The shot came from the *fourth floor*. Who shot Tim if it wasn't Betty, Reverend? *Who was the shooter?*"

The reverend shifted his gaze from the fire and looked into Mark's eyes.

"Why, Tim was the shooter, of course."

Chapter 8

Mark stared at the reverend for several seconds, then slowly closed his eyes. He didn't know if his friend was crazy, senile or both.

"Reverend," he sighed, "we were both there. We both saw him get shot."

"It was impressive, wasn't it?"

"Okay, I'm listening. Although I'm not sure why. What do you think happened?"

"First, let me ask a question."

Mark rolled his eyes. "Here we go. . ."

The reverend smiled in spite of himself. "Patience, Mark. I am in earnest. You initially said that two downstairs residents saw a yellow snake, and that various other tenants heard a car's backfire and a police siren. Is that correct?"

Mark searched his memory. "Uh, yes . . . as I recall."

"Let me suggest a different sequence to you. First the snake, *then* the siren, *then* the backfire."

Mark shrugged. "Whatever, Reverend. That's fine with me."

"It's an important point, Mark. Don't you know why the backfire happened *after* the siren? Haven't you guessed what the snake was?"

Mark was alternately exasperated and intrigued. Grudgingly, the latter won out. "Okay, Reverend, what was the snake?"

"It was a yellow *tape measure*. Tim was measuring the precise height of the window from the ground."

"But . . . why?"

"To insure that the trajectory of the bullet you found in the pavement matched the proper angle. I don't know what the correct angle is, but for the sake of discussion let's say it's forty degrees. If the bullet you recovered was embedded in the asphalt at, say, twenty degrees, that would raise suspicion, would it not?"

The reverend could see the wheels turn in Mark's mind. He continued with his theory. "All Tim needed to do was measure the distance from his car to the apartment building, then the height from Betty's window to the ground. After that, the calculation was a simple one, albeit necessary."

Mark was interested, but refused to show it. "Okay," he replied noncommittally, "*then* what happened?"

"First, let's fast-forward to the morning of the shooting. Did you notice that the curbside front tires of the two cars closest to the corner were moist?"

"No, Reverend. Only *you* notice things like that."

The old man smiled. "Perhaps you're right. In any event — assuming you'll take my word for it — doesn't that strike you as odd?"

"Not necessarily. Maybe the store owner cleaned his sidewalk with a hose. It happens all the time."

The reverend nodded. "That's what I thought. But, if you'll pardon the pun, that won't wash. If a merchant cleaned the sidewalk in front of his store with a hose, the front *and* rear tires next to the sidewalk would be wet. In this case, only the *front* tires were moist. How do you account for that?"

Mark shrugged. He had no idea, and he didn't think the

anomaly was worth discussing. Reverend Dean read his mind perfectly.

"The reason it's important is because a meter maid was across the street when the shooting started. I don't need to tell you how they mark cars in a two-hour parking zone."

That much, at least, Mark knew. Parking enforcement officers carried a long aluminum rod with a piece of chalk fastened to the bottom. The officer had a two-hour route, and she marked the front curbside tires of each car with the chalk. If, upon her return, she spotted a car with that mark on its tire, she knew that it had been there over two hours, and wrote a ticket.

"You're saying the wet spot on the tires was because someone washed the chalk off?"

The cleric nodded. "Exactly."

"And the relevance of this is. . .?"

"The relevance is that this means the cars had been parked there for over two hours. Why had Tim parked there for so long? And why did he also scrub the tire of the car in *front* of his car?"

"I give up. Why?"

"Because it was important to have both cars parked in those exact locations."

The old man struggled up from his chair and walked to the fire. "Here's what I think happened. Tim walked toward the street corner and pretended to see something at Betty's window. Then a shot rang out, and he spun around and hit the trunk of his car. Mark, you've seen more gunshots than I have. Surely you see a problem with *that*?"

Now that he mentioned it, Mark did. A .22 shot to the arm would never cause a grown man to spin around and fall to the ground. If anything — unless a bone was hit — the victim would think he'd been stung by a painful bee, rather than assume he'd been shot. At least until he saw the blood. Yet Tim had acted like someone in a Hollywood movie. He'd spun around and fallen backwards onto his trunk. Or . . . perhaps . . . he'd *thrown* himself against the trunk.

Mark dismissed the idea. "No, Reverend, I don't see a problem with that. He had a gunshot wound. People react differently when they're shot. We pulled a slug with *his* blood and *his* coat fibers from the pavement. We *heard* the shot."

"Those are good objections, Mark. Let me answer them by returning to the sequence I mentioned. The snake — which I've explained — then the siren, then the backfire.

"The backfire occurred some time after your tenant saw the snake. Why? Because the backfire wasn't from a car, but was a shot from a rifle. A rifle fired into the precise spot where you recovered the slug that supposedly hit Tim."

Mark leaned back and folded his arms across his chest. This was absurd, but he let the reverend continue.

"You may wonder why the rifle wasn't fired into the pavement as soon as Tim made his calculations. Because that's when a police car — siren blaring — raced down the street. Obviously Tim didn't want to be caught with a rifle on a downtown city street, particularly at that hour. Consequently, he had to wait until the police car — and whatever other vehicles might respond to that emergency — passed. Then he went into the street, made sure the angle of his shot lined up with the trajectory from Betty's window, and fired a bullet into the pavement. He had already parked his car in the spot necessary for the bullet to nick the rear bumper. Because the odds of finding that exact parking space the next day were prohibitive, he left the car there overnight."

Mark recrossed his legs. The old man's explanation was impressive, but only to a point. "It's . . . possible. But the wound, the sound. . ."

"Have you considered why Tim washed the tire of the car in

front of him? It's because *that* was his car, too. Or at least, a car he'd rented or borrowed. I'm sure you can determine which. In any event, what feature — more than any other item — do teenagers look for in a car?"

"A big engine?"

"I'm guessing that comes in second. What comes first?"

Mark began to shake his head, then stopped. "Speakers. A sound system!"

Reverend Dean smiled in approval. "Exactly. I don't know much about electronics, but that second car was between us and the apartment. All Tim needed to do was make sure the windows of that car were down — then remotely activate its speakers to play the sound of a gunshot — and we wouldn't be able to tell if the sound came from that car or the apartment."

"And the wound?"

"Ah . . . that. *That* will take some effort to explain. And even more to prove. Are you up for it?"

"What do you need, Reverend?"

The old man walked to the window, brushed aside the curtains, and peered at a series of rapidly approaching rain clouds. "You're going to need some old clothes," he replied, "and we need to hurry."

Chapter 9

Mark was changing clothes at his apartment when Reverend Dean told him where they were going. More succinct than usual, Mark had just one comment.

"No."

"It's the *only way*, Mark."

"I don't have the authority to do it, I don't know *how* to do it, and I certainly don't *want* to do it."

"You don't want to catch a killer?"

Mark sighed. "You know what I mean, Reverend. This is a wild goose chase, and I don't have the vaguest idea how to go about it."

"It can't be that complicated, Mark. Didn't you ever do it as a child?"

"No. And I can't believe that *you* did, either."

The reverend merely smiled. "In any event, don't you have a friend that works in the engineering department? Why don't you call him? *He* can help you."

"That's . . . not a bad idea," Mark admitted. "Clay would know what to do. But he'd need to call his supervisor to get approval."

"There's not enough *time*, Mark! You saw the rain clouds. It has to be done *now*. Believe me, when you find it, people will congratulate you, not condemn you."

"*If* I find it, Reverend! *If* I find it! If I don't, Clay and I will be reprimanded. If not *fired*. And he's got a wife and kid."

"I can't make you do it, Mark. Perhaps you know a better way to prove Tim's guilt."

"I don't know if he *is* guilty!"

"It's up to you, Mark."

Whereupon the reverend turned, walked into his friend's living room, and waited. Five minutes later, Mark emerged in tattered jeans, a stained sweatshirt, and foul-looking sneakers.

Reverend Dean had never been prouder of him.

"Clay's on the way," the detective said, grabbing a flashlight. "He'll meet us there."

Twenty minutes later, Mark stared with disgust at what the reverend had convinced him to enter: a manhole in a downtown sidewalk leading to the sewer. But this was no random manhole. It was less than ten yards from a stormwater grating in the curb where Tim was shot.

"Clay, this is Reverend Dean. He's, uh . . . assisting in the investigation."

Reverend Dean had been examining Clay since his arrival. He was in his late twenties, slightly overweight, with wild red hair and a pleasant smile. "It's a pleasure to meet you, Clay. Mark is fortunate to have a friend like you."

"No more fortunate than I am, Reverend. That's why I agreed to help. Not to mention I want to catch a killer."

Mark's expression, if possible, became more sour. But he said nothing. After introductions, the business-like Clay erected a protective railing around the manhole.

"You owe me. Big time," Mark whispered to the reverend.

"You're not doing this for me, Mark. You're doing it for Betty."

Clay pushed a metal rod into a slit in the manhole cover, turned the pole ninety degrees, and grunted as he pulled the heavy lid onto the sidewalk.

"I'm ready when you are," the engineer said, turning on his flashlight.

Mark sighed, shook his head, and stepped onto a cold, metal ladder. Within seconds both men vanished into the gloom.

Reverend Dean, standing guard on the sidewalk, looked at the sky. Lightning appeared several miles to the west. For the first time in his life he prayed that it *wouldn't* rain. And, far more importantly, that he hadn't jeopardized the careers of two fine young men.

Ten minutes went by. The moon vanished behind enormous rain clouds.

Fifteen minutes passed. A strong breeze picked up. Thunder shook the railing around the manhole.

Twenty minutes elapsed. To his horror, the reverend felt a sprinkle of rain on his face. But he still heard nothing from the sewer. What if he was horribly wrong? Mark would never trust him again. Not that it would matter, because Mark would no longer be a detective. Nor would Clay be an engineer. Fervently he prayed that he hadn't sent these courageous men on a fool's errand.

After twenty-five minutes he heard a boot strike the bottom of the ladder. That would be Clay. The cleric held his breath as the city engineer appeared.

Empty handed.

"Mark's behind me," he said without emotion. The reverend's heart sank. What had he done?

Ten seconds later Mark slowly appeared. Soaked from the ankles down, hair mussed, shirt soiled, and face smudged.

And carrying a plastic evidence bag!

"I don't know how you knew it was there, Reverend," the detective said with palpable relief, "but here it is. Now would you please tell me what it means?"

Chapter 10

As if it had been saving its fury for this exact moment, the storm suddenly unleashed an immense downpour. Mark helped Clay replace the manhole cover and all three men raced for the reverend's car. Sheets of rain lashed the vehicle as each man jerked open a door and threw themselves inside. The smell of wet wool and cotton permeated the vehicle as they caught their breath. The interior was lit only by a streetlamp, while outside the deluge sounded like a freight train. The combination produced an eerie, surreal effect.

"I've brought Clay up to speed," Mark said, raising his voice so it could be heard over the torrent. "He deserved to know what he was risking his neck for."

"I agree. And let me thank you again, Clay. This couldn't have been done without your help."

"This is my town, too, Reverend. It was worth it."

"So bring it home, Reverend. What does this," Mark shook the evidence bag, "mean?"

The retiree gazed fondly at the rain, turned on the car's heater, and collected his thoughts. "Mark, earlier you asked how Tim managed to feign his wound — or, at least, how he obtained it. Thanks to you and Clay we not only know the answer, but we can prove it.

"When we first saw him, Tim *appeared* normal. But there was nothing normal about him that morning. After he burned the cordite and left the brass in Betty's apartment, he broke into the unit across the hall, pulled Betty's door shut with the fishing leader, and made the phone call to her mother. Then he exited that unit via its fire escape — he couldn't use the door, because Mrs. Bunion was in the hallway — circled around the block, and appeared to be coming from a different direction when we saw him. Tim's "forgetfulness" — which caused him to backtrack to his car — was feigned, because it provided an excuse for him to turn around and look at Betty's window. We all followed his gaze, and that allowed him to trigger the sound system in the second car unobserved. After Tim threw himself onto his car's trunk, he slumped to the pavement."

The reverend stopped and cocked an eyebrow at Mark.

"By the way, the reason I was surprised when you said the lab didn't find further evidence on Tim's car was because there *should* have been blood from his wound on the trunk. But there wasn't. How do you explain that?"

Mark couldn't, and didn't try.

"In any event," the reverend continued, "after Tim slipped to the pavement, he was out of our line of vision. Once on the ground, he maneuvered his injured arm underneath the car, and—"

"Are you saying that Tim shot himself when he was under the car?" Mark interrupted.

"No. We would have heard the gunshot, and in any event he didn't have time. In fact, Tim shot himself *before* we saw him."

"*What*? That's impossible! Tim was smiling, strolling leisurely toward us . . . he wasn't wounded or bleeding!"

"Quite a performance, wasn't it? But keep in mind that we never saw him up close."

"So when *did* he shoot himself?"

"As soon as he left the vacant apartment. He couldn't risk shooting inside the unit, and if the wound were any older, the ER doctor would notice — from the inflammation, if nothing else — that it wasn't recent. I've examined the alley behind the apartment building, and it has very little traffic. It would be easy to erect a shabby cardboard shelter the night before — filled with pillows or other muffling material — climb in the next morning, fire a shot, then simply toss the whole shelter into a dumpster in the alley."

"But what about the slug we pulled out of the pavement? That had traces of *his* blood, fibers from *his* coat and chrome from *his* car."

"I'm sure it does. But it wouldn't be hard to arrange that. When he shot the bullet into the street, he made sure it passed through an identical jacket, dipped in blood he'd pricked from his finger. He also aimed the rifle so that it nicked his bumper. And he covered his arm with the duplicate jacket before he shot himself, so that you wouldn't find gunpowder residue. No doubt he wore gloves for the same reason."

"Reverend, you're forgetting something. There was no blood on Tim when we first saw him. But when I dragged him from the curb, his sleeve was bloody and had a hole in it. How do you explain *that*?"

"The blood was there, Mark, we just couldn't *see* it. After he shot himself, Tim concealed his bloody sleeve by loosely attaching a sleeve from the identical jacket over the sleeve of the jacket he was wearing. Thus, all he had to do after he slumped behind his car was pull the undamaged sleeve from his arm, and — *voilà* — we were presented with a wounded man wearing a bullet-ridden, bloodied jacket. But he did this *after* he fell from view. *That's* why there was no blood on the trunk."

"So this is. . ."

"Yes, Mark," replied the reverend, picking up the evidence bag. "This is the undamaged sleeve — lined with plastic, so no blood would seep through — that Tim pulled off his jacket and tossed down the curbside gutter."

"Reverend . . . I'm impressed. You—"

"Please," interrupted the old man, "do not congratulate me. I displayed no bravery. If the two of you hadn't acted when you did, the rain would have washed the sleeve away. You jeopardized your careers — you risked your futures and that of your families — to catch this killer. The public may never know of your courage, but whenever I think of heroes, I'll think of you and Clay."

Chapter 11

After Clay left, Reverend Dean drove Mark home. Although he'd come to a stop in his young friend's driveway, Mark made no move to leave the car.

"I've got a few more questions, if you're up for it."

"Of course, Mark. I'll answer if I can."

"*Why*, Reverend? Why would Tim do such a thing? Why not just divorce Betty?"

"You know him better than I do, Mark. Perhaps he'd found someone else and didn't want to wait. Perhaps he didn't want to lose the lifestyle he'd become accustomed to. I imagine you'll find out when you arrest him tomorrow."

The old man grew silent, and appeared lost in thought. He watched the windshield wipers slowly, rhythmically, sweep away the rain. Mark knew he was thinking about Betty Dearborn. They both were.

"Just one more question, Reverend. How did you know the sleeve was down there? Usually I can follow your logic, but tonight . . . I'm stumped."

"That's because I saw something you didn't see," the pastor allowed. "What gave me inspiration was an incident between a mother and a daughter."

The reverend described the scene where the mother wiped a mark from her daughter's shoe, was interrupted by a cell phone, which prompted the child to tug on her parent's sleeve.

"God works in wonderful ways," the reverend explained. "Consider the tableau He unfolded. In one brief episode, I saw — via a mother wiping a shoe — why only the *front* tires of Tim's cars were wet. I also saw — through a parent using a wireless phone — how it appeared that Betty called her mother. Finally, I saw — by a child pulling a sleeve — how Tim concealed a pre-existing wound." The reverend shook his head in admiration. "With God providing such clues, how could I *not* have seen what happened?"

As he exited the car and watched Reverend Dean drive cautiously away, Mark only half-agreed. Regardless of the source, he knew that most people would have missed the significance of the mother and child. Because two more things were necessary:

Reverend Dean's remarkable mind.

And the lonely old man's compassion to use it for others.

Murder on a Caribbean Cruise

Chapter 1

Reverend Thaddeus Dean's phone rang. Loudly.

This was rarely a good sign.

Anyone who knew Reverend Dean knew that he slept until ten in the morning. His friends knew it, his former congregation knew it, even Puppadawg knew it.

Nevertheless, someone felt it urgent enough to call at — Reverend Dean cracked an eye and looked at a clock on his wall — the unseemly hour of 8:00 AM. His clock didn't even register the time. It was a gag gift from his beloved wife, Emma, and it had no numerals where 6, 7 and 8 should be. It was made for people — like him — who felt that such hours should never be encountered in a wakeful state.

Yet here was someone who clearly believed otherwise. The reverend sighed, forced open both eyes, and reached for the phone.

"Hello?" mumbled the portly old man.

"Reverend Dean! I'm glad I caught you! This is Don Bracken! How are you this fine morning?"

Now the reverend was almost annoyed. There was only one thing worse than being woke up, and that was being woke up by someone cheerful. Still, he decided to be polite to his church's youngest deacon.

"Uh, f-fine, Don, fine. Is, uh . . . something the matter?"

"Well, yes and no. I've booked a cruise and I've got a new job. That's the good news."

"Congratulations." Given the circumstances, he thought his curt response was rather magnanimous.

"Thanks, Reverend. Unfortunately, the bad news is that I have to start the new job this week; which is when I booked my cruise. Worse, I didn't buy any travel insurance. So I was wondering: would you like to take my place on the cruise?"

"Well, Don, that's very gracious of you, but I'm sure I can't afford it, even if it were a short one."

"No, no, Reverend! I don't want you to *pay* for it! It's a gift! I just want to know if you'd like to go."

The reverend was now fully awake; the first time this had happened without caffeine in years.

"Don, that's . . . incredibly generous, but surely you can find someone who can reimburse you. I'm embarrassed to say that I don't think I ever could."

"Now, Reverend, you know that's not important to me, and never has been. In fact, the deacons have always felt bad that we didn't have enough money to give you a retirement gift. Why don't you look at this as an overdue present for a job well done?" The jolly deacon paused, then laughed. "It's hard to turn down when I phrase it like that, isn't it?"

Reverend Dean couldn't help but smile. Don had always been

one of his favorite church leaders, and he had a way of making anyone smile.

Even at eight in the morning.

"Don, I'm sure that even if I declined you'd pester me until I accepted," he teased. "But seriously, my friend, it's a very thoughtful gesture and I would love to go. I accept. Thank you."

"No, thank *you*, Reverend. Now I can start my job without feeling bad about the cruise. I'll come over this evening with the ticket and the other information you'll need. Is 6:00 alright?"

"It's fine, Don. So what is this new—"

"Can't talk any more, Reverend, I'll see you at six!"

The deacon hung up so abruptly that Reverend Dean didn't have a chance to learn about Don's new job. Well, he would have another opportunity this evening. With an excitement he hadn't felt in months, the old man literally hopped out of bed.

Reverend Dean learned more about his vacation after he met Don Bracken that evening.

The cruise departed from Miami in five days, and sailed around the Caribbean for an equal amount of time. The old cleric was rarely given to emotion, but he was almost bubbling with excitement by the time Don left. He immediately began a list of things to do before his trip.

First on the list was to arrange for someone to take care of his monstrous St. Bernard, Puppadawg. The elderly canine could tell his owner was excited, so he was animated as well. If the dog had known his master was leaving, he would have been far less sanguine. But for now he wagged his ponderous tail with vigor.

After the reverend completed his list, he took a rest in his old recliner and scratched Puppadawg's head. The reverend had never been on a cruise. It was one of several things he regretted not being able to afford for Emma. In fact — even though he hadn't mentioned it to Don — he'd almost declined his offer because it seemed somehow . . . *wrong* . . . to go on such a wonderful trip without his cherished wife. But Emma had passed away three years ago, and he knew that Don wouldn't accept that as an excuse. In fact, the deacon would have insisted all the more if he knew the reverend felt that way.

The old man shook his head. Although his intellect told him it was okay, he still felt a sinking feeling in his heart. He scratched Puppadawg a little more, then slowly shuffled to bed; far less happy than he'd been earlier that day.

Chapter 2

As the departure day arrived, Reverend Dean awoke earlier than he could ever remember, drove carefully to Sea-Tac International Airport, and took his seat on the plane. He was startled to find himself seated in first class. He'd never flown anything except economy his entire life. In fact, the only time he even thought about first class was when the stewards closed the curtains at the rear of the front compartment, blocking his view of the first class passengers. This always puzzled him. He thought that if first class passengers received better treatment, it was to the airline's benefit to let everyone see it, so that people would want to upgrade. The old cleric shrugged. In any event, after eighty years he would finally find out what it was like.

As the flight progressed, he had to admit that he enjoyed the increased room of a first class seat. It wasn't so much the increased legroom — the reverend had short legs — as it was the additional seat width. The realization that he needed this extra width annoyed him. He'd almost resolved to go on a diet — his third that year — when a stewardess approached him and asked if she could "lay his linen."

The reverend was stumped. He'd never heard such a phrase before. What was he supposed to do with linen? Not wanting to embarrass himself, he decided to play it safe.

"Ah, perhaps . . . later," he responded, hoping that it would, in fact, be available later — whatever it was. Fortunately, it soon became obvious that the stewardess was asking if she could lay a cloth on each passenger's tray in preparation for dinner. The reverend wasn't sure how this improved the meal, but — given his meager culinary skills — he was never one to turn down free food. His appreciation for first class was increasing all the time. The old man raised his hand.

"I think I'll have the linen after all," he whispered to the stewardess.

As Reverend Dean ate, he reviewed the only aspect of his trip that disquieted him. Don had explained that, several years ago, a dozen singles had enrolled in a cruise as a way of getting to know each other. The event was such a success that reunion trips occurred each succeeding year. However, as time progressed — and as people became married — fewer and fewer signed up for the event. This year it had only been Don and four others. All were in their thirties, and all except Don lived in Seattle. Reverend Dean shook his head. He feared that he would be as welcome as the plague. He knew that he didn't have to socialize with them, but he felt obligated to at least introduce himself and share a first dinner. After that, he'd have a better feel for whether he was welcome or not.

The flight was nonstop to Miami, so he indulged himself by watching an in-flight movie, then reading half of a mystery novel. Despite the long flight, he hadn't enjoyed himself this much in months. While aloft, he could read to his heart's content — without feeling that time would be better spent performing various chores. In fact, he was almost forced to read.

To the reverend, this was almost heaven.

* * *

After the plane landed, he collected his bags and took a shuttle bus to the pier where the ship was docked. As he and other passengers disembarked and waited for their luggage, he filled his lungs with the moist, salty air. The ocean had a smell that was utterly unique, and the reverend loved it. Involuntarily, a smile broke out on his lips.

The cleric examined the ship as he slowly walked up the gangplank. *The Angel of the Sea* wasn't as new, as large, or as shiny as the ships advertised on TV, but it was still the largest ship he'd ever boarded; over twice the length of the largest Washington state ferry.

A helpful porter directed Reverend Dean to his cabin — or "stateroom" as the man called it — but he was forced to seek help twice more before finding it. Until today, he'd thought that hospitals had the most confusing maze of hallways and passages. He now realized they had nothing on cruise ships.

Nonetheless, upon entering his room he was ecstatic. It had a private balcony overlooking the ocean! The old man dropped his bags, walked to the sliding glass door, and slid it open. The sun warmed his face as he stepped onto the lanai and listened to the seagulls. Since his youth, he'd always preferred rainy, stormy weather — he'd occasionally wondered what a psychologist would deduce from that — but even he had to admit this was perfect weather for a cruise.

Eventually he withdrew from the lanai and unpacked his suitcase. Don's brochure said that people usually brought more clothes than necessary for cruises, and advised travelers to pack accordingly. This wasn't a problem for Reverend Dean. He didn't have much to bring in the first place. Still, he'd attempted to be frugal in what he packed. As he finished hanging his clothes, he heard a soft knock on the door. Surprised, he quickly opened it. He was greeted by a pretty woman in her mid-thirties, with short, brunette hair.

"Hi! You must be Reverend Dean!" she smiled exuberantly, sticking out her hand. "I'm Carla!"

Surprise and confusion registered on his face as he took the woman's hand. All he managed to say was "hello," before she cheerfully interrupted.

"You're probably wondering who I am, and how I know who you are," she stated, rather than asked.

"Well—"

"I'm one of the 'Surviving Singles,'" she explained. "That's what we call our group now. Since I'm closer to Don than anyone else in our group, he called to explain why you came instead of him. Welcome!" she smiled.

The woman's grin was infectious. The reverend immediately liked her.

"It's a pleasure to meet you, Carla. But I'm curious; how did you know where to find me? There must me a hundred rooms onboard."

"Ninety-eight, actually. After years of cruising the same boat, you get to know trivia like that," she explained. "Anyway, we always have adjoining rooms, so I didn't have to knock on too many doors. Not that I *mind* knocking on doors," she digressed. "In fact — you won't *believe* this — one time there was a couple in this room, and they, they . . . uh . . . wait, you're a . . . a minister. Uh . . . never mind."

Carla blushed bright red. The reverend was amused, and tried to assure his new friend that she hadn't offended him.

"That's all right, Carla. After a few years, there isn't much that a minister hasn't heard. Nonetheless, I think we can leave the rest of your story to my imagination."

Carla was clearly relieved. "Uh, that's . . . that's probably a good idea, Reverend."

Reverend Dean smiled and changed the subject. "Have any of the other . . . Surviving Singles arrived?" he inquired.

"Nope," she replied. "We're the first. Do you want a tour? The only people who know this ship better than the Surviving Singles are the crew," she boasted.

"My dear, I would be delighted."

At the conclusion of Reverend Dean's tour, he understood why Don liked Carla. She was a thoroughly engaging woman, and reminded him of his niece, Susan. He had a delightful tour. As Carla escorted him back to his room, she invited him to dine with the Surviving Singles at six. Grateful for the invitation, he promptly accepted.

As he shut the cabin door, the old man glanced at his watch. It was only five o'clock, although it seemed later. Tired more from the flight than the tour, he laid down on the queen-sized bed. His hand involuntarily wandered to the other side to feel for Emma. The reverend was surprised; he hadn't done that in over a year. Reluctantly, he slowly pulled his hand away. Not wanting to become melancholy on the first day of his cruise, he quickly grabbed his mystery novel, bent a pillow under his head, and began reading.

Chapter 3

Reverend Dean arrived at the dining room at precisely six o'clock. The room was bigger, and more crowded, than he had anticipated. He scanned the room for several minutes until he saw Carla's hand waving at him. He navigated a maze of chairs as he moved slowly toward her corner table.

"Hello, Carla," he said cordially.

"Hi, Reverend! I'm glad you came. Here, I've saved you a seat."

He smiled around the table as he took an empty chair next to Carla.

"Let me introduce you, Reverend" began the exuberant woman. "Next to me is Gina Mayfield, beside her is Parker Deetz, and Lou Justin is on your left."

Reverend Dean smiled at each introduction, and quietly studied the group.

Roughly in their mid-thirties, Gina and Carla were the oldest of the group. Unlike Carla, however, Gina had platinum blonde hair, blue eyes with plenty of makeup, and an abundance of jewelry.

The men were in their early thirties, both approximately six feet tall. Parker ("Call me Park") Deetz, was tan and fit, with light brown hair, a broad smile and sparkling white teeth. Lou Justin, by contrast, was pale and thin, with dark brown hair, brown eyes and black glasses. Both men, however, could be considered handsome.

In fact, all four of the Surviving Singles were above average in appearance. The addition of a short, pudgy retiree, the reverend thought, dramatically skewed their table's average.

"Thank you for having me," he began sincerely. "As Carla may have told you, I've never been on a cruise before."

"Don't worry, Reverend, we'll take care of you," Gina grinned. "Speaking of which, our waiter's heading over here. Try the mahi-mahi. It's my favorite."

He followed Gina's advice, handed the waiter his menu, and glanced around the table. No one seemed inclined to say anything. Giving in to his natural curiosity, as well as an outgoing nature, the reverend leapt into the breach.

"You all know my profession — or what it used to be, at least — what do each of you do when you're not cruising?"

The reverend smiled benignly at no one in particular, looking to see who would volunteer. His demeanor, as it had during countless church meetings, soothed and calmed the table.

"Nothing special about what I do," began Lou. "I'm an engineer at Boeing, and have been for eight years."

"Defense or commercial?" the reverend inquired. Like most western Washington residents, he knew a little about Boeing.

"Commercial. Avionics."

Reverend Dean smiled in acknowledgement.

"And — going from a huge corporation to a small business — I run a costume company," trumpeted Park. "Started it three years ago, and now employ four people."

"I've always admired people who are willing to risk failure, and strike out on their own," confessed Reverend Dean. "I admit I'm on the risk-averse side, myself."

"Well, it was scary for the first eighteen months," Park conceded, "but now it's going okay. Still, I wouldn't mind having the retirement benefits of a Boeing employee."

Park winked good-naturedly at Lou, and everyone smiled.

"I know Carla is an administrative assistant with the county," the reverend continued, "what about you, Gina?"

"*I*," explained Gina, tossing her head back theatrically, "am a woman of leisure."

The entire table laughed.

"Indeed?" the reverend smiled, going along with what was obviously an in-joke. "And how did you arrange that?"

"I married rich and divorced young," she stated baldly, without a trace of self-consciousness.

"I'm trying to get her to teach me how to do it," ribbed Carla, "but she won't give any pointers."

"I'm afraid some of us are just born with these skills," Gina sighed. "It's a burden I've learned to accept."

Carla rolled her eyes and smiled at Reverend Dean. The cleric didn't know what to say so he said nothing. Gina was apparently telling the truth, but was so shameless about it that everyone found it amusing. Despite her entertainment value, however, the reverend worried for anyone who might develop feelings for her.

A worry, it turned out, that was terribly well founded.

Nonetheless, the rest of evening progressed enjoyably, and his fear that he wouldn't mesh with the group never materialized. One reason he wasn't a "fifth wheel" was because the foursome wasn't paired up in any way he could discern. Carla was obviously just friends with the men, and although Gina might have a relationship with Park, it was somewhat veiled. This confused him. If it existed at all, why conceal it? There was also some connection between Gina and Lou, although the engineer didn't appear to be Gina's type. Nonetheless, each member of the group was highly engaging and pleasant. Reverend Dean quickly understood why Don met with the "Singles" year after year.

After dinner, as he walked slowly to his stateroom, the old man felt relieved. Four new friends and an ocean cruise. How could this not develop into a vacation of a lifetime?

Chapter 4

Two days later, the cruise ship made the only stop on its itinerary: Grand Cayman Island. Although it was scheduled to dock at 8:oo AM, the reverend was sound asleep when he was roused by a loud banging at his door. Alarmed by the noise, he quickly grabbed his bathrobe and confronted the knocker. He was met by his four newest friends.

"Reverend, we've gotten to know you over the past two days, and we've come to a decision," Gina said sternly.

"We think you should go to Hell."

Rarely had the reverend been more surprised. For one of the few times in his life, he was speechless.

Then everyone — except the reverend — started laughing.

"Judging from the expression on your face," Carla giggled, "Gina was right; you have no idea what we're talking about."

"Well . . . I must confess. . ."

"Come on, Reverend, get dressed. Everyone's going to Hell, you might as well too," Lou grinned.

"Ah . . . *everyone's* going?" the reverend asked, still more asleep than confused, although that was rapidly changing.

"Alright, we've had our laugh," smiled Park. "Reverend, there's actually a town named Hell on the island. It doesn't have much more than a post office — mainly so tourists can get their letters postmarked from Hell — but it allows everyone to tell their friends that they've been to Hell and back."

"Well," the reverend admitted, "if I was still preaching, this *would* make a good sermon." Almost awake, he smoothed what little hair was on his head and smiled. "In any event, if you'll give me fifteen minutes, I'd be honored to accompany you."

The reverend quickly completed his toilet, then tried to determine what clothes to wear. His young friends were all fashionably dressed, with designer shirts, trendy shorts, and expensive athletic shoes (were there any other kind nowadays, he wondered?). The reverend was slightly embarrassed as he examined his meager options. Since everyone was in shorts, he decided to wear the only pair of shorts he owned: knee-length, red & green plaid, Bermuda shorts. He might not be in Bermuda, he mused, but at least he was in the Caribbean. Almost touching the bottom of his shorts were his knee-high white athletic socks. Emma had broken his habit of wearing dark dress socks with his shorts, but the shorter, ankle-length socks were still too new for the reverend's tastes. Finally, he selected one of two golf shirts he'd brought along: a short-sleeved, all-white, cotton pique.

The reverend was ready.

In deference to Reverend Dean's age, the group decided to take a cab to Hell, then walk back.

Upon arrival, the quintet was decidedly underwhelmed.

In addition to the post office, there were numerous craggy, dolomite and limestone formations — which apparently inspired the town's name — but virtually nothing else.

"Well," recalled Park, surveying the scene, "my last girlfriend told me to go to Hell, but I had no idea she was that upset."

The reverend's friends laughed, and — since it was obvious

there was nothing else to do in Hell — Gina told him about their next stop.

"Grand Cayman has the Caribbean's only sea turtle farm," she explained. "You can see everything from babies, to turtles that weigh 600 pounds. It's just five minutes from here. Are you game?"

"I would *love* to see them, Gina."

The reverend was more excited than Gina knew. Ever since he was a boy, he had been interested in giant sea turtles. His mother, who had lived on the Carolina coast as a child, told him that when female turtles dug a hole and laid their eggs in the sand, she would hop onto their shells and ride the plodding beasts back to the water. She jumped off when they hit the ocean, however, because as soon as they entered the sea, the turtles transformed themselves into strong and graceful swimmers. Of course, such childhood fun was now illegal. The reverend had mixed feelings about that. On the one hand, he agreed that turtles and their habitat should be protected; on the other hand, it seemed a shame that such harmless fun — his mother never touched the eggs — was now prohibited.

Several minutes later they entered the farm. Lou took off his Seattle Mariners baseball cap and wiped his brow. "Well," he observed, "it's just five minutes away, but this place is hotter than Hell."

The reverend smiled and sighed at the same time. He feared he would be hearing these jokes all day. Nonetheless, he enjoyed himself immensely at the turtle farm. He had no idea the giant, gentle creatures could live as long as a hundred years. He had known, however, that they'd almost become extinct; so he was pleased that the farm released five percent of its stock into the sea each year. He was less pleased — although he understood the economic need — that some turtles were harvested for local restaurants. Thus, when they stopped for lunch at the farm's café, he ordered a hamburger instead of turtle soup and sandwiches.

Bellies full, the group left the café and began their trek back to the ship. The journey paralleled the shoreline — known as Seven Mile Beach, although it was just 5½ miles long — and was enjoyed by all. Three miles into the trip, however, the reverend began to tire.

"I hope you won't think me rude," the old man began, "but I confess I don't usually walk this far in one afternoon. There's a stand that rents umbrellas and chairs on the shoreline just ahead, and that would be a perfect way for me to take a rest. I apologize for being so out of shape, but this way I won't slow any of you down."

"Reverend, there's no need to apologize," replied Lou. "What good is a Caribbean vacation if you can't relax on a beach? Actually, I'd join you, except Park and I have a reservation on the ship's driving range."

The reverend had read about *The Angel of the Sea*'s golf range in the ship's literature. It featured biodegradable golf balls, so the balls wouldn't obstruct the blowholes of whales; where many balls surprisingly — and often fatally — ended up.

"I'd sit with you, too, Reverend, but bingo starts in an hour, and I can't miss that," Carla smiled. "How about you, Gina?"

"Actually, if the Reverend doesn't mind some company, I'd like a little rest, too," she said, turning to the reverend.

"My dear, I would be delighted for the company."

As the group split, Reverend Dean rented a spot with a large umbrella and two chairs. Gina moved her chair in the sun to increase her tan, while the reverend — well under the shade of the giant umbrella — fanned himself with a brochure. For several minutes neither spoke, as they listened to the waves and watched the various bathers and beachcombers. Eventually Gina turned to the reverend.

"Reverend, do you mind if I ask you a question?"

"Of course not, Gina. What's on your mind?" He had already guessed that Gina wanted to talk about something.

"All this talk about hell, Reverend . . . do you believe in it?"

"I assume you mean after we die; not where we visited."

"Yes," she smiled.

The reverend collected his thoughts as he removed his shoes and socks.

"Well, if you believe the New Testament — which I do — then it's very difficult to dismiss the existence of hell. Jesus spoke of it, the apostles wrote about it, and they all described it as a real, literal place. And — it goes without saying — a place to avoid."

"But, Reverend, how can a loving God send anyone to hell?"

"He . . . He doesn't, my child. At least not in the way you may think. *We* do."

Surprised, Gina's expression invited the old man to explain.

"It isn't so much that God sends someone to hell, as it is that we tie His hands and send ourselves to hell by our rejection of Him. It breaks His heart to see anyone push Him away, but — since He's given us free will — we have that horrible choice. The alternative would be for Him to create automatons with no voice in the matter; something a loving God won't do."

He wiggled warm sand between his toes, and tried to think of an example.

"It's a poor analogy, but compare it to a son who's just turned sixteen. Although his parents know he might get in a car wreck — through some bad decision on his part — they still allow him to get a driver's license, because loving parents know that's a part of growing up. It doesn't mean they want him to die. Taking the analogy further, Christ can come to earth and die for us — just as a driver ed teacher can tell a student to look both ways — but that doesn't insulate us from the tragic consequences if we don't listen."

The reverend was thankful that no one overheard him compare God to a driver education teacher.

"But why would He actively torture us for making the wrong decision?"

"Gina, it may help to remember that, perhaps foremost, hell is the absence of God. People often think of hell as fire and brimstone; and the Bible does use fire to describe hell. But it also describes hell as utter darkness.3 Since God is commonly described as light,4 I think the real torture won't be fire, but the absence of God.

"Let me illustrate. Many years ago, Emma, my wife, developed an internal infection. It spread horribly, and for several days her doctors thought that she would die. During that time, when I feared I might lose her, I experienced a horrible, empty feeling that was far worse than any physical pain I've ever known. The pain was caused by the fear I might lose her; that she would be absent from my life. Sometimes, I think that's what hell is like. Not so much a physical pain by fire, but a far worse *spiritual* pain, caused by the absence of God." The reverend paused, then added, "I think, once someone has experienced His total absence, they'd much prefer the fire."5

"Well, okay; maybe I can understand why Hitler, or Ted Bundy, would go to hell. But most people are okay, Reverend. *I'm* okay. How can God send *normal* people to hell?"

"Gina, as far as humans go, you're more than okay; you're delightful," he assured her. "But you're thinking of heaven as something to be earned. And, if it was, you're not holding yourself — or anyone else — to a very high standard. You know, until our generation, it never occurred to anyone that they *deserved* heaven; almost everyone admitted they were sinners. That isn't how modern people view themselves. Today, we think we're too good for hell, and — if God contradicts us — then He's not just unfair, He's wrong. No one wants to use *God's* standard: which is holiness."

"But no one's *perfect!*"

"You're right. That's why He made salvation a gift, instead of something we earn. But every gift has to be accepted. If we say, 'Sorry, no thanks, I'll find my own way to heaven,' then we're demanding His absence; which brings us back to the defining characteristic of hell."

Gina looked intently at the reverend, then slowly turned her head and watched the waves. They were silent for several minutes.

Suddenly she glanced at her arms and legs.

"Eek! Reverend, if I lay out any longer, I'll roast. Let's finish our talk on the way back. Are you rested?"

"Enough to accompany you, my child."

Chapter 5

After an enjoyable walk, Gina and the reverend arrived back at *The Angel of the Sea* just before 4:00. The ship left George Town promptly at 7:00 PM, so passengers could watch its leisurely departure while they ate a late dinner. After eating, as was their custom, the Singles went their separate ways. Lou, however, pulled Carla aside before she could leave.

"Carla, do you have a minute later on? I'd like to talk to you about something."

The woman was surprised, but agreeable.

"Of course, Lou. When do you want to get together?"

"How about in fifteen minutes. At the left, uh . . . port side of the ship, near the lifeboats."

"Fine. What's the matter? Is something wrong?"

"Actually, something may be right. But that's what I need your advice about. I want a woman's opinion," he grinned.

Carla smiled in relief. "Well, you know me; I'll give my opinion about anything. See you in fifteen."

Carla was as good as her word, and after changing her clothes met Lou at the appointed place. Lou was still wearing the sunglasses, shirt and athletic shoes he'd worn during their day trip, although he'd changed into slacks after dinner. The sun had just set, and it was still very warm. The gentle breeze created by the ship's progress felt good to both of them as they strolled the walkway.

"Okay, mystery man, what's up? What couldn't you say during dinner?" Carla teased.

Lou smiled back. "What would you say if Gina and I got back together?" he asked, apparently pleased with himself.

Carla was surprised. Not only had Gina and Lou broken up almost two years ago, but — as far as she knew — Gina was now involved with Park.

"Well, that's . . . that's wonderful, I guess. I mean, whatever makes you and Gina happy. But what about—"

Lou jerked his head behind him. "Blast! Who *is* that guy? What does he *want*?"

Carla turned around, but saw nothing. "Who are you talking about?" she asked, somewhat concerned.

"This weird guy has been following me around for a couple of days now. But it's only when I'm out on deck, never inside. Haven't you seen him? He's tall — taller than I am, at least — and muscular, and has this long, dark beard."

"That doesn't ring a bell, and I'd remember someone who looked like that."

"Well, I'm tired of it. He saw me looking at him, so he ducked behind those lifeboats. Wait here. I'll be right back."

"Lou, are you sure you should? No one's nearby, and it's getting dark. Let's get Park."

Lou's manly pride seemed offended.

"No, no, I'll be alright. I can take care of myself. I don't need you, Park or anyone else."

"Okay," Carla said, obviously unconvinced. "I'll be right here if you need . . . uh, I'll be right here."

Lou strode to an area between two stacks of three lifeboats apiece. Carla vaguely recalled there was enough room for two people in that space, but not much more.

Although she couldn't see them, she heard Lou ask the man who he was and why he was following him. She heard the men speak in low voices, but couldn't discern what they were saying. After a minute she gave in to her curiosity, and inched toward the area where they were talking.

"Carla! Come—"

Lou's yell abruptly stopped. Carla ran toward the men, ready to help her friend.

She was stunned to see a tall, bearded man in waders leaning over the guardrail, striking something. Then she saw Lou's legs hanging on the other side of the railing! The man was trying to push him overboard! Before she could move, the brute grunted and gave a massive downward strike with his fist. Carla heard a sickening thud. Leaning further over the railing, the man chuckled as he looked into the ocean. Only then — clearly satisfied with his actions — did he face Carla. The horrified woman could now see the entire guardrail. Lou was no longer there!

Thinking quickly, Carla grabbed a life preserver, pushed past the man and threw it overboard. But before she could take another step, the beefy man grabbed her hair, jerked her from the railing, and punched the courageous woman in the middle of her face. Carla flew across the deck and slammed into the side of the ship. The animal had broken her nose as easily as he had thrown Lou overboard. As she slid down the wall, Carla watched groggily as the creature walked to the nearest door, threw it open and vanished inside the ship. The last she saw of him — even in the fading light — were the monster's demonic blue eyes glaring at her as he disappeared through the hatch.

Fortunately for Lou, Carla never lost consciousness. She pulled herself up and ran to the railing. There was no sign of her friend. Holding a hand to her bloody nose, she raced to the bridge.

"There's a man overboard!" she exclaimed, bursting into the room.

The officer took one look at Carla then glanced at the helmsman.

"All stop. Initiate overboard procedure," he ordered calmly, then turned to Carla. "When did this happen, and on which side of the ship?"

"Maybe, maybe a minute ago," she guessed. "On the . . . uh . . . on *that* side of the ship," she pointed.

"Name and age of the person overboard?"

"Lou Justin. Age thirty-two. But a man hit him first — before he threw him overboard! I threw out a life preserver, but he may not be conscious!"

"Was the man who hit your friend the same person who hit you?"

"Yes."

Even though she was gagging on her own blood, Carla was reassured by the officer's manner. It seemed that nothing rattled him.

"Jackson, please escort this lady to sickbay. I'll handle rescue. While you're there, please get all details regarding this incident. Particularly the identity of whoever," he looked at Carla's nose and clenched his jaw, "did *that.*"

After Carla left, the officer paged the captain, and the crew began its much-practiced procedure. Surprisingly, however, the captain instructed his officer to proceed without him. At that moment he had his own problem.

"Tell me what she said again?" Captain Riley asked one of two crewmen. All three were standing in front of a stateroom door.

"She called and said we shouldn't blame ourselves for what she was going to do," the man replied. "Then she hung up. We tried to call her back, to see what she meant, but no one picked up the phone. We were on our way to her cabin when we saw you."

"Is this her stateroom?"

"Yes, sir."

The captain rapped fiercely on the cabin door.

"Ma'am, this is Captain Riley. I'd like to speak with you, please."

There was no response. The captain knocked again.

"Ma'am, I'm afraid I must speak with you. Please open your door immediately."

The captain and both crewmen listened intently. There was no sound. The captain sighed in impatience.

"Ma'am, if you don't open this door, we'll be forced to open it ourselves. Please open this door *immediately*."

Ten seconds later, the captain turned to the nearest crewman

"Do you have the master key?"

"Yes, sir."

"Open it."

Although the key worked and the knob turned, the door wouldn't budge. First one crewman, then the other, tried to force the door, but neither met with success.

"Do you know where the battering ram is?" asked the captain.

"Yes, sir."

"Get it."

The battering ram was a very heavy metal cylinder, two feet long, with two handles on each side of the canister. It allowed two men to hold the ram — one on each side — swing it into a door, and break any lock in the process. The captain had never seen a door withstand more than two swings. Out of breath from running with the heavy object, the crewman arrived with the ram.

"Do it."

One swing.

The door barely budged.

Two swings. The door held, but the ram punched a crack in the space above the knob.

Three swings. The door held, but the crack became a fist-sized hole. The men threw down the ram, and the nearest crewman peered into the cabin.

"She's got a door stick, that's why."

The captain swore. Although it went by many names, a door stick was nothing more than a hollow metal tube, usually one inch in width, with a rubber foot on one end — in order to grip the floor — and a rubber fork on the other end. The forked end of the stick is jammed under a doorknob, and it was virtually impossible to open a door using the device without destroying the door. The crewman reached in, grabbed the stick, and pulled it away from the doorknob in disgust.

The captain pushed open the remnants of the door. He wasn't a religious man, but he prayed the woman was alright. Or at least not too far gone. Perhaps they were in time.

They weren't.

Gina Mayfield was hanging from a noose thrown over her bathroom door. Her lifeless, unblinking eyes greeted the men as they entered the room.

"Oh, my poor child," the reverend whispered behind the men.

"What are *you* doing!?" The captain turned to a crewman. "Get him *out* of here!"

From his room across the passageway, Reverend Dean had been roused by the battering ram. Alarmed, he'd opened his door and watched the captain and his men enter Gina's room. Highly concerned for his friend, he had followed the men inside.

As the crewman approached, Reverend Dean raised his hand

and said just one word.

"*Stop.*"

The crewman froze. Reverend Dean had a way of asserting authority that belied his short, plump appearance. Even the captain was silent.

"I know this poor child. She was my friend. I was one of the last people she spoke with."

The second crewmen had already lowered Gina's body and laid it on the floor. The reverend walked to the body, caressed the woman's hair, turned her head, and held her hand.

"Then maybe you know why she decided to kill herself," asked the captain, regaining his voice.

The reverend looked up in surprise. "Why do you think that?" he inquired.

"Fifteen minutes ago, she called the bridge and told us that we 'shouldn't blame ourselves' for what she was going to do. Then she barricaded her door, and . . . well, you can see for yourself."

"Indeed I can." The reverend gently turned his friend's head again. "And that's how I know this poor woman did not kill herself. She was murdered."

"How can you—. Who *are* you, anyway?" the captain sputtered.

"My name is Thaddeus Dean. More important, however, is the fact that I am a deputy sheriff."

Some time ago, the reverend's friend, Detective Mark Small, had deputized him when the entire Dark Pine police force came down with the flu. The reverend had spent several fascinating nights patrolling the town with his friend. Since the deputization had never been revoked, the reverend was still, technically, a deputized sheriff.

At least he assumed so.

In any event, he saw no need to inform the captain that he was also a reverend, with absolutely no law enforcement training. Thus, before anyone could question his qualifications, the old man pointed to the dead woman's head.

"Look at my dear friend's neck," he quietly instructed the captain. "What do you see?"

"Rope burns. Anyone who hangs themselves has them. What's your point?"

"Rope burns, yes. Anything else?"

"*No* Deputy Dean, I *don't* see anything else. What is it you want me to see?" Like any captain, he didn't like to be lectured on his own ship.

The reverend quickly explained. He needed the captain as an ally.

"When anyone hangs themselves, the rope burns encircle the neck — as you pointed out — but they also create an upside down 'V' where the rope meets the knot. That's because the rope must be hung on something, and when it's hung, it pulls the knotted portion of the noose upward; thus creating a rope burn in that shape.

"But if someone has been *strangled*, the rope marks will be quite different. Since there's nothing pulling the knot up, there will be no inverted 'V,' and the rope burns will be straight across the neck; because the murderer has tightened the rope *horizontally*.

"You can see that poor Gina suffers from a completely horizontal rope mark. She was viciously murdered, then hung on the bathroom door to make us believe it was a suicide."

The captain shook his head in disagreement. "Well, I don't have your experience, but the neck marks aren't that clear to me. It could go either way. More importantly, if it isn't a suicide, who put that door stick under the doorknob? The bathroom is too far away for her to have done it, and no one can prop a door stick behind a doorknob from the outside. And there's no other way out of this room — unless you think someone climbed out that nine-inch porthole."

The reverend walked to the porthole and tried to open it. It wouldn't budge.

"Save yourself the effort, Deputy. It's for viewing purposes only. It doesn't open. It never has."

The reverend sighed and walked to the broken door. Bending down, he closely examined the doorknob. Given the abuse it suffered under the ram, it was surprisingly sturdy. He rattled it a little, then — to the captain's amazement — sniffed it. A quizzical look clouded his face.

"Captain, what does this smell like to you?" the reverend inquired, standing and pointing to the mechanism.

Nonplussed, the captain bent over gave a cursory smell to the doorknob.

"It smells like a doorknob, Deputy. Nothing else."

Surprised, the reverend looked at the nearest crewman.

"How about you, sir? Do you smell anything?"

The young man bent down and carefully sniffed the whole apparatus.

"Ah, you're going to think I'm crazy, but it smells like. . ."

"Yes?" prompted the reverend.

"Well . . . like a mint julep."

The captain rolled his eyes and swore.

"Uh . . . sorry, sir." The embarrassed crewman blushed and stared at his feet.

The annoyed captain faced the reverend. "Regardless of how it smells, can you tell me how anyone other than the dead woman could prop this stick under her door?"

"No," he admitted. "But I stand by my conclusion. This is a murder scene — not a suicide. As such, I urge you to keep this room exactly as it is until we reach . . . where *are* we going, now that we've had this tragedy?"

"Still Miami, Deputy. We're in international waters, so we're outside the jurisdiction of the Grand Caymans. We could go to Key West, but if you're right — and this is a murder — the Miami P.D. will be more experienced than the Key West locals. One of our boilers is out so it'll take us a while to get there, but we'll still make port within forty-eight hours."

Chapter 6

As Reverend Dean was exiting Gina's room, the officer of the bridge, Richard Harold, approached the captain. He was accompanied by a soaking Lou Justin, covered in an equally wet blanket.

"Sir, we've recovered the passenger who was pushed overboard. He's shaken, but safe."

"He was *pushed*?"

"Yes, sir. Fortunately he was close to the ship, and we were able to pick him up immediately. A woman who tried to assist him was also attacked."

"Where is she?"

"Sickbay. Her nose was broken."

"Good Lord. Can they identify their attacker?"

Harold frowned, then repeated Carla's description of the attacker.

"Perhaps you've seen someone like that, sir, but it doesn't fit any passenger I've seen. We've either got a stowaway," the officer said, "or someone who was wearing a disguise."

"Make a thorough, but discreet, inspection of the passengers," the captain ordered. "I haven't seen anyone like that either, but there's no harm in checking. If you don't find anything, make a complete search of the ship. At the very least, I want to eliminate the possibility of a stowaway."

"Yes, sir."

"What's the name of the woman involved?"

"Carla Jumonville."

"I'll go and see her straight away." The captain turned to one of the crewmen. "Seal this room and let no one in. Rich, walk with me to sickbay. I'll update you on what's happened down here."

"Captain, if you don't mind, I'd like to accompany you," asked the reverend. "Carla is a friend of mine."

"Suit yourself, Deputy."

The visit was both uninformative and uneventful, except when Reverend Dean told Carla of Gina's death. Initially the captain tried to stop him, but after the old man explained they were friends, he was allowed to proceed. After several minutes of comforting and hand-holding, the doctor stated that Carla needed to rest, and the men left sickbay.

"Rich, assuming the passenger in cabin 66 isn't a suicide, do you think the man who did this," the captain jerked a thumb toward sickbay, "could be our murderer?"

Harold shrugged. "If not, it's a big coincidence. We've never had anyone thrown overboard before, much less murdered."

"I agree. I want to talk to this Lou. . ."

"Justin," said the reverend helpfully.

The captain stopped and examined the old man.

"I suppose he's a friend of yours, too?"

The reverend allowed a hint of a smile. "Yes, in fact."

The captain sighed. "Well, come on then."

Two minutes later, Harold knocked on the door of cabin 67, which was promptly opened by Park Deetz. Unlike Gina, Carla or the reverend, the two men shared a cabin.

Before anyone could speak, Reverend Dean gently cleared his

throat and spoke to the captain.

"Lou and Park," he gestured to the men in the cabin, "are friends of both Carla and Gina," he cautioned. "If I may. . .?"

The captain nodded.

"Lou, how are you, my son?" he asked gently.

"I'm okay now, Reverend. But I was half-unconscious when I hit the water; if Carla hadn't thrown that life preserver. . ."

The old man nodded. At least there weren't two deaths.

"Lou, Park, we have some tragic, terrible news." The reverend paused to let the men prepare themselves. "I'm afraid that Gina has . . . died."

"What!?" Lou exclaimed. "How? When? *What happened!?*"

Park merely covered his face in his hands. Reverend Dean glanced at the captain before responding.

"It isn't conclusive, but we think she may have been murdered," the reverend said.

"You've got to be kidding! Who? Why? We're in the middle of an ocean! We were going to. . ." Lou stopped and regained his composure. "Tell me what *happened*!"

The reverend brought both men up to date. Park said nothing, while Lou remained incredulous.

"We'll make Miami in forty-seven hours," the captain explained, "but you can see why we need to ask a few questions before then, particularly of Ms. Mayfield's friends. Mr. Justin, I don't have any questions for you, since you were overboard at the time of the death."

The captain turned to Park, who wasn't pleased by this shift in attention.

"Mr. Deetz, where were you between. . ." the captain looked at Harold for guidance.

"Eight and 8:30," completed the officer, using civilian time rather than "20:00" and "20:30" to avoid confusion.

"Why that time?" asked Deetz.

"Mr. Justin was thrown overboard at approximately 8:00. We received the phone call from Ms. Mayfield at 8:15. We arrived at her stateroom at 8:25. So I repeat: where were you during this time?"

"I . . . I was strolling the decks. I wasn't doing anything in particular."

"Was anyone with you during this time?"

"N-no. I was alone." Park became angry. "But that doesn't mean I killed her!" he exploded. "I loved her! We were seeing each other!"

This last comment elicited a curious look from Lou. The captain held up both hands in a gesture of appeasement. "No one is accusing you of anything, Mr. Deetz. We're just asking questions. Surely you can understand that."

"I . . . I suppose," conceded Park.

During the captain's questions, Reverend Dean took the opportunity to examine the men's cabin. Fortunately, their closet doors were open. Each man had a full wardrobe, albeit stocked in different ways. Park had far more clothes, while Lou owned shoes for every conceivable occasion. Thoroughly unenlightened, he leaned back and peered into the small bathroom. Each man had staked out one side of the sink with his toiletries. Nothing unusual there. In fact, the arrangement extended to the dresser in the bedroom. It was obvious who used which side. The right side held Lou's glasses, while Park's area harbored expensive cologne. Both sides had a wallet, watch, sunglasses and loose coins. Trying not to seem nosy, the reverend bent over for a closer exam. He saw nothing out of the ordinary. Mentally shrugging, he turned his attention to the captain.

"Please accept my condolences for all that's happened. I promise that no stone will be left unturned as we investigate these events. In the meantime, if you remember anything you think is important, please contact me."

As the captain walked out, the reverend shook Lou's hand; less as a goodbye than in an effort to comfort the man.

"It looks as if you were smudged with grease during your rescue," he observed, looking at the base of Lou's thumb. He pulled a handkerchief from his back pocket. "Let me get it for you."

Lou shrugged and gently pulled his hand away. "That's okay, Reverend. There's some tissue right here," he said, wiping the smudge off and tossing the tissue in a wastebasket.

The reverend turned to shake Park's hand. The man abruptly looked at his fingers, rubbed his left wrist and silently took the reverend's hand. Reverend Dean studied Park, then addressed both men.

"If either of you need me, I'll be in my cabin."

"Thank you, Reverend."

The old man gently shut the door, then joined the officers in the passageway outside the cabin.

"'Reverend?'" mimicked the captain. "I thought you were a deputy!"

"Oh," the old man replied, with a twinkle in his eye, "that too."

Chapter 7

It was late at night. The moon was almost full. The reverend had been sitting on his lanai for hours, staring at the ocean as it lapped slowly by. This horrible, tragic affair utterly mystified him — on several levels.

First, who was this mysterious man who attacked Lou and Carla? He assumed the man — and it had to be a man, at that size — was in disguise. But what was his motive? If he harbored some hatred for Lou, why wait until a cruise to kill him? Surely it was harder to kill someone with a roommate — on a ship full of people — than it would be at Lou's home in Seattle.

Unless . . .

Unless the attacker learned something on the ship that he hadn't known before. That would be the obvious explanation. But, as far as the reverend knew, Lou didn't know any man onboard except Park. And what in the world could Park have learned in the last few days that would prompt an attack? And, more importantly, was this the same person who killed Gina? Intuitively the reverend believed the incidents were linked. But even if Park had attacked Lou and Carla, why would he kill Gina?

The reverend considered the obvious motives: love, money and revenge. He had little data regarding the second category, except that Park supposedly owned a business and appeared well off. He tentatively crossed that motive off his list.

Love could be a motive, but attacking Gina, Lou and Carla certainly wouldn't prompt that emotion in any of them. So much for that category.

That left revenge. But for what? What had Park learned that could prompt such murderous rage? Had Gina been unfaithful? That might do it. Unfaithful with Lou, perhaps? That sounded even better. And perhaps Carla just got caught in the middle. That was the most plausible explanation.

Of course, there was also an almost unbelievable explanation — and there were facts to support it — but it seemed too absurd to contemplate. The reverend put that possibility aside for the time being.

Of course, all these theories assumed that Gina's death was a homicide. The reverend was reasonably certain of this, but he wouldn't stake his life on it. But if it *was* murder, how did the killer jam the door stick under the doorknob? He had examined the door very closely. There were no air vents, no bottom panels that could be unscrewed, no hinges on the outside, and no space between the door and the weatherboard. Just a door, a doorknob and a lock. Even the doorknob screws were on the inside of the door.

And a door stick jammed firmly against the door from the inside.

Annoyed at what he believed to be his slowness, the reverend rose, entered his cabin and closed the lanai door. If Gina's room had an outside deck — like his stateroom — that would make everything much simpler. But it didn't. He glanced at the clock by his bed. One-thirty AM. The pudgy cleric slipped on his shoes and headed toward the ship's dining room.

No one needed to tell the reverend that he was a little

overweight. He patted his waistline. Perhaps more than a little. Consequently, when he learned that the ship had a 24-hour buffet, he resolved to avoid that area whenever possible.

Thaddeus Dean's willpower lasted until he discovered that the buffet served banana pudding.

Even then, he might have resisted if the pudding had been warm or runny. Unfortunately, it had been made exactly as God intended: cold and thick, with ripe bananas and whipped cream topping. That first night, he'd visited the buffet three times. Exhibiting what he believed to be admirable resolve, however, he restrained himself to one visit per night the following evenings.

This evening he entered the dining room, strolled to the desert bar, and selected the nearest bowl. It was moist and warm from a recent washing. He filled the bowl, walked to the table nearest a window, and dug his spoon into the thick dessert. While he enjoyed three of his favorite things — banana pudding, the night and the sea — he momentarily forgot about the tragedy afflicting his friends.

But when he returned to his cabin, put on his pajamas, and pulled the cool sheets over his body, Reverend Dean's wonderful mind was as frustrated, and as sad, as it was before his snack.

Chapter 8

The next morning Reverend Dean awoke at 10:00, dressed, and headed to the dining room for breakfast. In Dark Pine, he tried to eat healthful breakfasts of cereal and fruit, but — like the banana pudding — he found a morning meal of warm biscuits, crunchy bacon and cheesy eggs was just too attractive to resist.

So he didn't.

As was his habit, he bought the day's newspaper to read during breakfast. He was halfway through his meal when he happened to look at a woman flossing her teeth at the next table.

Some people might have been offended by this breach in etiquette. But — this morning at least — Reverend Dean wasn't one of them. In fact, he laid the paper in the middle of his eggs as he stared at the woman in amazement. A dark spot slowly appeared in the sports section as it absorbed the moisture from the food. Why hadn't he thought of that before? That would explain half the problem! But could he prove it? The reverend abruptly left the table and shuffled to the bridge. Minutes later, out of breath, he knocked on Park and Lou's door. Park answered. Lou was just entering the room from their deck.

"I thought I'd see how the two of you were doing this morning," the reverend said, catching his breath.

Lou merely shrugged.

"As good as can be expected," Park said morosely.

"We've walked the whole ship," Lou said with frustration, "looking for the man who attacked me, and probably killed Gina. He's nowhere to be found."

"Have you seen Carla?" the reverend inquired. "I assume she's out of sickbay now. I was going to visit her in a few minutes."

"We just left her, Reverend. She was up early this morning, but now she's taking a nap. It might be better to wait an hour or two."

"Of course," the old man agreed. "By the way," he asked, turning to Park, "could I trouble you for some dental floss? I'm afraid I left mine at home."

"Sure, Reverend." Park rose, went in the bathroom, and emerged with a plastic container of floss. The reverend examined the case. After opening it, he turned to Lou.

"Lou, I hate to be a bother, but this isn't waxed. It's really the only kind I can use. Would you have any, by chance?"

"No problem, Reverend," he laughed good-naturedly, "It's on top of my bag in the bathroom. Help yourself."

"So mine's not *good* enough, eh, Reverend?" teased Park.

Reverend Dean smiled back. He was glad that Park hadn't taken offense. The old man entered the bathroom, flipped open the floss, pulled out a string, clipped it off and snapped the case shut. Upon reentering the bedroom, he bent over the trashcan to deposit the used floss.

"Ah, much better," he beamed. "Next time, Park, I trust you'll know what to bring," he teased. Park chuckled as the old man left his friends and entered the passageway. The reverend bumped into the captain before he had a chance to close the door.

"Ah, Captain. Thank you for coming to see me. The reason I wanted to talk to you is because I have a suggestion."

"Yes?" the officer responded warily.

"I think you should place tarps over and around the lifeboats where the attack on Lou occurred. We know the police will find Lou's fingerprints on the railing, but who knows what prints they may find in and around the lifeboats themselves."

The captain appeared skeptical. "I suppose that's possible, but we're making port tomorrow, and the crew's pretty busy. I won't be able to spare a man until. . ." the captain looked at his watch, "until oh-dark-hundred."

"Excuse me?" the reverend asked.

"I'm sorry. Military slang for first thing in the morning, before dawn," explained the captain.

"Ah. Well, that will have to do," he replied with disappointment. Before he could plead any further, however, Mr. Harold entered the passageway and began talking about a missing life preserver, a damaged deck chair, and several rowdy passengers in cabin 56 who were suspected of other acts of vandalism. As he left, Captain Riley turned toward Reverend Dean.

"Anything else, Deputy? I've got a ship to run."

"No, Captain. Thank you for your time."

Although the moon was full, dark clouds obscured most of its light. The deck was surprisingly silent as a figure dressed entirely in black crept toward the port lifeboats. It was hard to tell if it was a man or woman.

Upon reaching its destination, the mysterious shape unrolled a paper bag. It crinkled so loudly that the figure froze, looked around, and listened before proceeding. After a motionless minute, the silhouette gingerly pulled a brush and water bottle from the bag, tossed the sack over the railing, and squirted some liquid onto the brush. The shadow spent several minutes scrubbing the exterior of the middle lifeboat.

Once that task was complete, the figure quietly removed the

boat's tarpaulin cover, scrubbed the interior of the boat, then silently replaced the canvas. Apparently tired from its work, the shape took a long swig of water before it heaved the bottle and brush into the ocean.

Then a second figure stepped quietly from a well-concealed shadow.

"I'm afraid your work was for nothing, my child. The captain has already switched the lifeboats," the reverend said softly.

Startled, the figure stood motionless, staring at the solitary old man.

"You shouldn't have come here, Reverend. If I hurt my friends, what makes you think I won't hurt you?"

A searchlight burst to life, bathing the figure in light.

"Because he's not alone," snapped Captain Riley, perched on a deck above the reverend with four other men. "Rich," he ordered, pointing at Lou Justin, "arrest that man."

Chapter 9

The following morning, the captain, first officer Harold, Carla, Park and the reverend were gathered in the captain's conference room.

"From what I saw and heard," the captain began, "Lou Justin appears to be our man. What I don't know is how you figured it out. Now that we're all here, give us the details, Deputy."

"It really isn't that mysterious," the reverend began, with genuine humility. "There were several clues to suggest that Lou wasn't pushed overboard in the way we'd believed. But until I could explain how someone could jam a door stick under a knob from the outside, it was just idle speculation."

"So how *did* he do it?"

The reverend picked up a battery-operated screwdriver, borrowed from the ship's maintenance department, and approached the conference room door.

"May I?" he asked the captain.

"Be my guest."

In under a minute, the reverend had removed the doorknobs from both sides of the door. He then pulled three feet of dental floss from his pocket, folded it in half — so there was a loop on one end, and two loose ends on the other — and fed the looped end through the hole where the doorknobs used to be and out the other side of the door. Leaving the floss hanging on both sides of the hole, he then loosely reattached both doorknobs.

"The trick," he explained, "is to leave the screws attaching the doorknobs just a little loose. If you tighten them too much, the floss can't be extracted; but if they're not tight enough, the loose doorknob will attract attention. If they're just a *little* loose, however, any shakiness will be attributed to the use of the ram."

Grabbing the door stick used in Gina's cabin, the old man inserted its forked top within the loop of floss hanging inside the door, and gently wedged the stick under the interior doorknob. Then — grabbing the loose ends dangling *outside* the door — he pulled the floss taut. As he did so, the door stick wedged firmly under the doorknob. Maintaining his grip on the floss, the reverend gently pulled the door several inches.

The door stick followed the door the entire distance.

"Once shut, to remove the floss, you just pull on either end hanging outside the door," he explained, gently pulling on one end of the floss. As he spoke, the floss surrounding the door stick gradually shortened, while the floss outside the door gradually lengthened. Eventually, he held the entire length of floss in his hand.

"*Voilà.*"

The entire procedure, including explanation, had taken less than two minutes. The group was amazed. No one would have guessed the old man had such a nimble — and devious — mind.

"This also told me *who* committed the murder," the reverend continued. "Captain, you may recall that I asked your crewman to smell the doorknob in poor Gina's room."

"Yes, I remember. He said it smelled like a . . . a whiskey sour, or something."

"Actually, he said it smelled like a mint julep. Same liquor, different mix."

"Whatever, Deputy."

"It's a vital distinction, Captain. Park, would you do me a favor and smell the inside of this doorknob? Carla's closer, but I don't think she'll be smelling anything for a while," he explained, referring to her broken nose.

Park bent over, and took a whiff of the lock.

"It's mint," he admitted.

"Well then, what *caused* it?" blurted the captain. "It obviously isn't liquor."

"No it's not," the old man replied. "It's mint-flavored floss. But I've put the floss in my pocket. So what's Park smelling?"

No one ventured a guess, so the reverend continued.

"Captain, do you see this small dollop of residue at the edge of the inside knob? It's easy to miss; it's about the size of a pinhead."

The captain bent over and examined the doorknob.

"Why, now that you mention it . . . I do. What is it?"

"You'll find a similar residue in the exact location on Gina's door. It's *wax*."

"From the floss, when you pulled it out!" exclaimed Carla. "That's why you can still smell the mint!"

The cleric nodded.

"So when I discovered that Lou had this type of floss, I took a closer look at his alibi. At first I was stumped, but then it dawned on me. Lou was quite ingenious. What he'd done was erect a double-alibi for himself. First, he tried to make Gina's death seem to be a suicide. However, if that didn't work, he had a fall-back plan: he would be overboard when the murder occurred."

"But, Reverend," Carla objected, "he *was* overboard."

"That's true, my child. But *when* was he overboard? There were several clues that indicated it was later than we thought."

"For example?" inquired the captain.

"For example," answered the old man, "do you recall the words of your first officer when he reported that Lou had been rescued? No? I do, because they struck me as peculiar. Mr. Harold said, 'he was close to the ship,' and that he was 'able to pick him up immediately.' Didn't that strike you as odd?"

By now, the captain realized the old man was shrewder than he looked, so he suppressed his desire to ridicule a civilian's grasp of maritime matters.

"Ah . . . I believe so," hedged the captain, "but why don't you give me *your* idea."

"Of course, Captain. My idea is this. We were traveling between twenty-five and thirty miles per hour — eighteen to twenty knots, in your lingo — when Lou was supposedly thrown overboard. It took Carla approximately one minute to reach the bridge, and at least another minute for Mr. Harold to slow the ship and lower a rescue boat. At the speed I mentioned, we should have traveled at least a mile beyond the spot where Lou was thrown overboard. How, then, could he be 'close to the ship?'"

"Well, er, I assumed that Ms. Jumonville — given her injuries — was not completely lucid. And . . . uh, I assumed that Rich was speaking broadly."

"Of course. That would be a natural reaction," agreed Reverend Dean. "Your chief concern would be the recovery of your passenger, not the location where he was found."

"Quite right," replied the captain.

"And that explanation occurred to me, as well," the reverend admitted. "That's why I found Park and Lou's cabin so interesting."

"Excuse me?" inquired Park.

"Well, Lou's side, at least," he clarified. "For example, did you notice that Lou's wallet and watch appeared absolutely normal? In other words, *dry*? This suggested that either he was lucky that he wasn't carrying them when he was attacked, or that he had removed them before he leapt overboard.

"For that matter," continued the reverend, "did you notice his sunglasses on the dresser? He was wearing them when he met Carla. Yet even when he was struck in the face — and fell twenty feet into the ocean — they not only survived, but remained in normal condition."

The old man looked for a chair and sat down. The ordeal had drained him, and he was tired.

"Of course, it's possible that Lou put them in his pocket after he fell overboard, but he claimed that he was 'half-unconscious' when he landed. So how do we explain the sunglasses?" He shrugged, then continued. "I suggest they were either an oversight, or that Lou didn't want to lose them. Since I presume they were prescription sunglasses, that's understandable. Regardless of the reason, however, they shouldn't have been there."

The captain was annoyed. He'd been in the cabin as well, but he hadn't seen — or more accurately, hadn't deduced — any of these discrepancies.

"Finally, I noticed a tiny smear of oil on Lou's hand. It didn't mean anything at the time, but after I experimented with the doorknobs, I noticed a smidgeon of grease on my hand, as well. And grease — as you know, Captain — doesn't come off in sea water.

"In fact," the cleric mumbled, rummaging through his pockets, "I palmed Lou's tissue when I pretended to throw his floss away. Now where is it. . .

"Ah! Here it is," exclaimed Reverend Dean, flourishing the dirty tissue as if it were a flag. "I imagine the Miami Police might find this interesting if they compare it to the grease in the doorknob."

"Reverend, this is all well and good. But you're forgetting

something, aren't you?" asked Carla.

Reverend Dean raised an eyebrow in surprise.

"I *saw* him fall overboard, Reverend! Explain *that!*"

The old man was embarrassed.

"Ah! I'm so sorry my dear!" he apologized. "I become forgetful in my dotage. But to answer your question, in reality you saw very little. You did, however, *assume* a great deal."

Carla, annoyed, folded her arms across her chest. "Reverend, I was *there*. I know what I saw!"

"Then let's go through it together, my dear. Did you see the bearded man before Lou told you he'd hidden behind the lifeboats?"

"Not . . . really."

"Did you see Lou when he called out to you?"

"Well, not at that precise minute. . ."

"Did you see Lou at all — except for his legs hanging over the railing — before the large man struck downward, supposedly sending him overboard?"

Carla sighed. "No," she admitted.

"And what happened when you tried to look over the railing, my child?"

"That's when he hit me."

"Exactly. He didn't want you to look in the ocean and discover that no one had fallen overboard. Because that would have led you to the truth: that the bearded man was Lou."

"But . . . that's impossible! He was taller than Lou, he had blue eyes, he was dressed differently. . . Reverend, he wasn't the same man!"

"I agree he wasn't the man you thought you knew, Carla, but let's think this through. What was Lou wearing when you last saw him? Sunglasses, yes?"

"Nothing's unusual about that, Reverend."

"I must disagree, Carla. I suggest that at dusk — when the sun has set — they *are* unusual. This indicates that he had a specific reason for wearing them."

"But what in the world would that be?"

"He was hiding the fact that he was wearing blue contacts."

Carla was stunned. She'd never even considered that possibility.

"And there's one other anomaly," offered Reverend Dean. "After dinner, Lou changed from shorts into slacks. Have you wondered why? The temperature was still very warm."

"Okay, you've got me; what *was* the reason?" asked Park.

"The long pants provided something for Carla to see through the railing; so she would assume that Lou was hanging overboard."

The captain was shaking his head. "I don't follow. Walk me through this from the beginning."

"Of course, Captain. The previous night, Lou had hidden special clothes — as well as a dummy, dressed in the same clothes he would wear the next day — in one of the lifeboats. After meeting Carla, he feigned seeing a stalker, and told her to wait where she was. This allowed him to change clothes in private. First he pulled on a padded, long-sleeved shirt, then applied a fake beard. He already had on contacts. Finally, he stepped into a pair of waders. By the way, has anyone wondered why an attacker would wear waders?" inquired the reverend. "Obviously he wasn't going wading in the middle of an ocean."

No one responded.

"I believe he wore waders for three reasons. They concealed most of his body, they almost certainly had heel-lifts to make him taller and — most importantly — he could step into them in mere seconds.

"After dressing, he screamed for Carla, who naturally assumed that Lou was in trouble. But when she arrived, all she saw were

Lou's pant legs — and even then, just for an instant — before the bearded man threw his punch and let them go."

Carla was stunned.

"I . . . I *guess* that could have happened," she admitted. "But that's so . . . so bizarre! Especially when Lou had just told me that he and Gina were back together!"

"Another ruse, my child. A lie to throw off any suspicion that might attach to him. And it made sense, because only poor Gina could refute it."

"What did he do next?" Captain Riley asked, trying to keep the conversation on track.

"Tragically, he went directly to Gina's room. I think we know what happened next."

"Well, *I* don't," the captain objected. "Ms. Mayfield called the bridge herself, and expressly told my officer that we shouldn't blame ourselves for what she was going to do. How do you explain *that*?"

"It was simple enough," the old man replied with a sad expression. "Did she respond to any questions?"

"No."

"Did she say anything else?"

"No, she hung up."

"Had your first officer spoken with her before, so that he would recognize her voice?"

"Ah . . . I don't think so," responded the captain, looking at Richard Harold. The first officer shook his head "no."

"Perhaps you see where I'm going," Reverend Dean kindly suggested. "To further support the hoax that Gina committed suicide, Lou picked up her phone after he killed her — knowing you could identify the cabin of the caller — and played a recorded message into the phone. The recording could have been made by any woman, and I'm sure Lou told whoever made it that was some sort of joke. After that, he positioned the door stick as I've shown, left the room, and discretely jumped overboard; probably from his own lanai."

Almost as an afterthought, he added, "By the way, Captain, I believe I can explain your missing life preserver."

"What are you talking about? You mean it wasn't the college kids in cabin 56?" he asked skeptically. "What makes you think that?"

"You'll recall that Carla — very bravely, I think — threw a life preserver to Lou when she thought he'd been forced overboard. This provoked Lou's anger, and he struck her. His rage was quite genuine, because if — once you picked him up — he didn't have a life preserver, that might arouse suspicion. If your men looked for it, there was no way he could explain why the preserver Carla threw was a mile away. Consequently, he took a second preserver from a different area of the ship before he leapt overboard."

"Well I'll be. . ." murmured the captain. "Deputy, I don't know why I ever doubted you."

Reverend Dean, rather embarrassed, looked out the window.

"But how did you know that Lou would scrub the lifeboats last night?" asked Park.

The old man shrugged.

"Once I realized where Lou hid his disguise, I knew his fingerprints would be on the inside of one of the lifeboats. So I arranged for the captain to meet me outside of Lou's room, so I could suggest — within earshot of Lou — that he secure the lifeboats. That was why Lou had to scrub the boats last night. He wouldn't be able to explain why his fingerprints were on the inside of one of the boats."

"But that doesn't explain *why* he did it," wailed Carla. "Gina was his *friend*. We *all* were."

The old man sighed. Not out of impatience, but of sadness.

Sadness in the fallen human condition.

"As you say, my child, you were his friends; far more than I. So I can only venture a guess. You said that Lou told you that he and Gina were getting back together. The obvious inference, therefore, is that they were previously involved. I don't know how it ended, but obviously Gina preferred Park. Lou might have tolerated that for a while — hoping Gina would change her mind — but as her relationship with Park progressed, Lou must have decided that if he couldn't have her, no one could."

The reverend struggled up from his chair and walked to the conference room window. It was a brilliantly sunny day. Just like the day they'd left port. But so much had changed, in such little time. Last week, he hadn't thought it possible that he could be surrounded by water, yet be so unhappy. He turned, shuffled to the door, and quietly left the room.

Chapter 10

As they disembarked several hours later, Reverend Dean was struggling with his luggage when a strong hand reached out and steadied his suitcase. It was Park.

"I know we've said all our 'goodbyes,' Reverend," the man said softly, "but I wanted to pass something along, for whatever it's worth."

"I would love to hear it, Park."

"Gina and I were close — as you obviously know — so it was natural for us to talk before dinner. When the two of you returned from the beach, she said she had a long talk with you, and that she'd made a decision; the biggest one of her life. She said that she'd tell me about it after dinner, but . . . but she never got the chance. Do you know what she was talking about, Reverend? Do you know what she meant?"

The old man's eyes filled with tears. But he was also smiling — for the first time since their last dinner with Gina.

"Yes," he replied. "I do."

The reverend couldn't stop a tear from rolling down his cheek.

"It means that I'll see her again."

Murder at the Lord's Table

Chapter 1

The house was small by modern standards. It was over fifty years old, and contained a living room, kitchen, utility room, den, two bedrooms and — its one extravagance — two bathrooms; one that was part of the original house, and one that was clearly an addition.

The smallest bedroom had been converted to a miniscule study, overflowing with books, magazines, files and newspapers. All rooms were furnished tastefully, but clearly on a limited budget. Nevertheless, the overall feel of the home was traditional, warm and solid. A bulwark against a harsh and unforgiving world.

The grounds were unusual for such a modest house. The front yard existed in name only, but the back yard was surprisingly large. Only a monstrous St. Bernard, currently slumbering on a worn mat in the utility room, explained the need for such space.

Inside the brick Tudor home, an unusual conversation was taking place.

"Thaddeus, have you ever seen an . . . an angel?"

The owner of the house, the retired Reverend Thaddeus Dean, neither laughed at, nor dismissed, the question. He'd known Pastor Steve Ragsdale too long to take such a question lightly.

"Well, Steve, not that I know of," the reverend admitted, "but the Bible indicates that angels can assume the form of men, so I'll probably never know this side of heaven."[6]

"I . . . I may have, Thaddeus," the pastor said nervously. "In fact, my entire congregation may have. Two Sundays ago, in open church."

Reverend Dean leaned forward in fascination. "Please, go on."

It was winter, and the fireplace hadn't yet warmed the den. But Steve Ragsdale was perspiring. This event, whatever it was, had clearly upset him.

"It happened during the Sunday service, just as I was preparing to read a passage from the New Testament. As I rose and approached the lectern, a man sitting in the front row stood and pointed a finger directly at me."

The pastor took a handkerchief from his back pocket and dabbed his brow.

"Did you know this man?" Reverend Dean gently asked.

"No, I'd never seen him before. Nor had anyone else. I *call* him a man, but you have to appreciate how he *looked*, Thaddeus. He was dressed completely in white. A perfectly pressed, white, three-piece suit, a white starched shirt, a white silk tie, even a white leather belt and shoes. But that wasn't all. He was *big*. At least six foot six, broad shouldered, tapered waist and . . . and dazzling blond, almost white, hair. I've never seen anyone like him."

Reverend Dean was impressed. He'd never seen anyone like that, either.

"What happened when you approached the lectern?"

"As I said, the man slowly rose, planted his feet, and pointed a finger directly at me. Obviously I delayed my Bible reading, wondering what he was going to do."

"And?"

"Thaddeus, he looked me square in the eye and quoted a verse from scripture! In a deep, bass voice, he said,

> "A man should examine himself before he eats the bread and drinks the wine. For anyone who eats and drinks unworthily eats and drinks judgment on himself. For this reason many of you are weak and sick — and some of you have died."

Reverend Dean was intrigued. In all his years as pastor, he'd never encountered anything like this.

"What happened next?"

"He turned, strode majestically down the aisle and walked out of the building. Everyone was too dumbstruck to follow him."

The bewildered pastor mopped his brow and continued.

"I tried to make light of the situation, and quipped that 'I didn't know we had another preacher in the congregation,' but it was unnerving."

Reverend Dean stroked his chin in thought. "That man's — or angel's — declaration," he said softly, "it's Corinthians, is it not? Pretty faithful rendition, if memory serves."

"It's 1 Corinthians 11:28-30. It's a unique paraphrase, but it definitely conveys the spirit of the verses."

"I grant you his appearance was imposing, Steve, but surely it's unlikely that he was an angel."

"That's what I thought. Until last Sunday."

Reverend Dean cocked an eyebrow. This was becoming more intriguing by the minute.

"Last Sunday, John Snead — our music pastor — rose to give

the New Testament reading. We conduct all pastoral duties in alphabetical order, and it was his turn. But this time — instead of an angel — sitting in the front row was another man dressed very differently. He wore a beige robe, brown leather sandals, and had long, dark hair. Thaddeus," the pastor gulped, "he looked just like Jesus!"

Reverend Dean knew there was no description of Jesus in the Bible. Aside from the fact that he was circumcised, and presumably shared a physiognomy common among Jews, nothing was definitively known. Of course, that didn't stop artists from portraying Christ in every manner possible. Thus, modern man had an "image" of Jesus, even though it was based on nothing except an artist's imagination.

Reverend Dean didn't insult his friend by stating this. Steve Ragsdale knew the Bible as well as anyone. Still, old images were hard to break. And in any event, the image of a robed, sandaled visitor in a front pew would unsettle any pastor.

"What happened next?"

"As John approached the lectern the man rose — just like before — and raised his hand. But this time he didn't point to the person at the podium. Instead he pointed at me again! He said:

> "A man should examine himself before he eats the
> bread and drinks the wine. For anyone who eats
> and drinks unworthily, eats and drinks judgment
> on himself. For this reason many of you are weak
> and sick — and one of you *will* die."

Reverend Dean immediately noticed the new ending. "This no longer sounds like a prank," he said quietly.

"Thaddeus, you haven't heard the end of it."

The jittery pastor swabbed his brow with a now damp

handkerchief, took a gulp of lukewarm coffee and continued.

"Just as before the man turned and left. But this time, instead of leaving by the main exit, he walked into the pastors' study! This was too much to bear so our youth pastor, Rick Taylik, ran into the room after him."

The pastor threw down his handkerchief and scanned the room, as if searching for words to describe what happened next.

"Thaddeus, when he entered the pastors' study, the room was empty! *There was no one there!*"

Reverend Dean paused in surprise, then asked the only logical question.

"Doors?" he inquired.

"Yes, one to the outside," admitted the pastor, "but it's a double deadbolt — you must use a key even if you open it from the inside. But even if he had a key he didn't have time to use it! Rick was there less than five seconds after the man entered the study. And there was no place for him to hide! Thaddeus, I'm at my wit's end, and we celebrate communion next Sunday!"

"Calm yourself, my friend, calm yourself," Reverend Dean said reassuringly. "What do your assistant pastors make of this?"

"Rick and John are perplexed, of course, but not overly concerned. That doesn't surprise me. They're levelheaded, solid pastors; good at what they do. Of course, we have our theological differences, but you're well aware of that."

Indeed the reverend was. Steve Ragsdale was a rarity: an evangelical pastor in a highly liberal denomination. The reverend knew his friend didn't look for theological fights, but he didn't back down from them, either. More than once, this had created tensions. Not just with the junior pastors, but with the denominational hierarchy, as well.

"In any event, Thaddeus, you're the expert in matters like this. No, no, don't shake your head. Over the years you've had a knack for solving strange problems, and the fact that this happened in church makes it even more up your alley. So here's my question: will you attend our morning service next Sunday? It would mean the world to me."

"My friend, you couldn't keep me away."

Chapter 2

The following Sunday Reverend Dean awoke earlier than usual. After drinking several cups of coffee, and scanning the front section of *The Times*, he retreated to the bedroom. He shuffled through his closet with some embarrassment.

Reverend Dean had never accumulated much money. Not because he was a spendthrift, but because his church was a poor one, and the congregation could never afford more than a nominal salary. It helped that he and Emma had never had children, but occasionally they had little money even for essentials — like clothes. The old man always regretted that he couldn't dress Emma in the finery that she deserved. She had never complained, of course, but he always felt inadequate — as the family breadwinner — that he couldn't provide more.

This paucity extended to his suit collection. When he'd been an active pastor he'd always worn vestments, which concealed the limited number, and threadbare condition, of his clothes. As he studied his three suits — all over nine years old, and one over twelve — he regretted that he didn't have something more appropriate for his friend's church.

The reverend shook his head in annoyance. That was how the material world thought, he reminded himself. It didn't matter to

God, and he knew it wouldn't matter to Steve Ragsdale. He smiled and selected his youngest suit, together with a faded tie so old it was almost back in style.

Reverend Dean parked in the church parking lot, and pulled on a pair of wool gloves before exiting his car. It was bitterly cold, but out of habit he parked at the far corner of the lot so that visitors could park near the entrance. He waddled slowly to the double-glass doors, pulled one open and entered the bustling church narthex.

The reverend knew his friend would be too busy to speak until after the service, so he strolled around the crowded first floor of the church. One of the assistant pastors was serving coffee, which Reverend Dean gladly accepted. After finishing the surprisingly good drink, he found his way into the sanctuary and sat in the middle of the front row. He didn't expect anyone unusual to show up, but — if they did — he wanted to get as close a look as possible.

The old man was glad he'd arrived early. Although the service didn't start for fifteen minutes, the sanctuary was almost full. He had no idea if this was due to the mysterious visits, or simply the church's normal attendance.

However, there did seem to be a . . . *buzz* among the congregation. Reverend Dean had spoken at many churches over the years, but he couldn't recall anything approaching — was it just his imagination? — the level of *anticipation* which appeared to permeate the crowd.

As the pastors entered, he tried to recall what little he knew of Steve's assistants. He'd actually met the music director, John Snead, two years ago. He reminded the reverend of Ichabod Crane, from *The Legend of Sleepy Hollow*: tall, gaunt and always fidgeting. Reverend Dean almost smiled. The young man seemed to have found his calling as a choir director, because it allowed him to keep moving — at least when he was directing the singers.

However, Ichabod Crane had never dressed as well as this man. His tasseled Gucci loafers, crisp Ralph Lauren shirt, expensive wool slacks, and designer blazer made the reverend's clothes look particularly shabby. The old man subconsciously pulled his overcoat around his suit.

The youth director, Rick Taylik, was five foot nine (almost as short as Reverend Dean) and rather dark-complected. Part Venezuelan, if the reverend recalled correctly. He'd earned a Masters in Divinity from an Ivy League school, and was highly regarded in the church. Unlike John Snead, however, Rick Taylik's attire was more low key, though no less tasteful.

It was now 11:00. The service began smoothly enough, although the reverend could hear a pin drop when Rick Taylik rose to give the New Testament reading. To the relief of most — and perhaps the disappointment of some — the reading proceeded without interruption.

Now it was time for communion.

Several men and women came forward to accept the wafer plates, and the group efficiently circulated the trays throughout the congregation. Simultaneously, Pastor Snead — presumably because he was the closest of the pastors — picked up a plate, removed a wafer, and passed the tray to Steve Ragsdale. The senior pastor took a wafer and handed the plate to Rick Taylik. The youth pastor took a wafer for himself, rose, and set the plate on a shelf inside the dais. It was the practice of this denomination to eat the wafer simultaneously, so the congregation waited until Pastor Taylik stood and approached the podium.

"This represents our Lord's body, which was sacrificed for us," the pastor said, raising the wafer to his mouth. The pastors and congregation swallowed the bread as one.

Was it his imagination, or did Pastor Ragsdale look pale after eating the wafer?

The group which circulated the wafers approached the altar to accept new trays stocked with cups of grape juice. Pastor Snead picked up a tray and Rick Taylik again approached the lectern.

"Just as we eat the bread together to symbolize our unity in Christ, we drink the cup separately to symbolize our individual relationship with Him."

Steve Ragsdale, looking shaky, accepted a cup from the tray, and passed the plate to the standing Pastor Taylik.

"This represents the blood shed for our sins." Taylik said, raising a cup to his mouth and drinking it.

Pastor Ragsdale also raised a cup and drank. As the plates circulated among the congregation, the senior pastor grimaced.

As the ushers collected the trays, the pastor gripped his stomach.

Then, to the horror of the congregation, Steve Ragsdale groaned, doubled up and collapsed to the floor!

"I'll call 911!" Snead cried, running to the pastors' study. Kneeling by the stricken man, Rick Taylik frantically tried to tell if Steve needed CPR. After confirming he was breathing, and that his heart was beating, he held the pastor's hand as the entire church waited for the medic truck. He didn't need to ask the parishioners to pray. He knew they were doing that already.

The medic van arrived ten minutes later. By that time Steve Ragsdale had stopped breathing and was not responding to Rick Taylik's furious efforts at CPR. The EMTs took over the procedure, but eventually acknowledged the worst.

Pastor Steve Ragsdale was dead.

As the aid truck slowly carried the body away, the congregation was in a state of shock. Lacking a clear leader, Pastor Taylik took the podium.

"Brothers and sisters, we have encountered a . . . crushing, horrible blow this morning. I'm at a loss for what to say except this: go to your homes, and pray for those who grieve for our beloved pastor. As we find out more in the coming days, we will keep you informed. God bless you all."

As the pastor descended from the dais, a hysterical woman rushed to meet him. "Pastor Taylik, is this a divine judgment on Pastor Ragsdale? Was this a supernatural—"

"*Mrs. Rupert,*" the pastor interrupted her. "We know no such thing. All we know is that our Lord took Steve to be with him. To assume anything else would do the memory of our pastor a grave disservice."

The woman, looking doubtful, assumed a martyred silence and walked grudgingly away. Upon hearing Taylik's response, those who'd approached with the same question turned and walked slowly out the door.

Reverend Dean seized this opportunity, as did Pastor Snead.

"Pastor Taylik, it's horribly difficult to meet someone under such circumstances, but I am Reverend Thaddeus Dean. I was a good friend of Pastor Ragsdale, and in fact attended this service at his request."

"Yesss," the man nodded in slow recognition, as he accepted the reverend's hand. "Steve mentioned you often, including his visit to you last week."

The reverend also extended a hand to Pastor Snead, although he didn't know if the pastor would remember him. "Hello, John. I'm sorry to see you again under such tragic circumstances."

"This is all such a shock." The music director shook his head in disbelief. "I . . . I don't even know what to say."

The old man laid a hand on the pastor's shoulder. He didn't know what to say, either. They had lost their senior pastor, and Reverend Dean had lost a dear friend.

"I . . . I need to get away from here," Snead said to no one in particular.

"I would like to ask a personal favor, if I may," Reverend Dean injected, showing obvious embarrassment. "I understand the need to get away, but might we get away together? Unlike the two of you, judging from your rings, I have no one to talk to at home. It would mean a great deal for me to spend a little time with individuals who knew my good friend as well as I did."

Perhaps anticipating their reaction, Reverend Dean added, "Just for a short time, I promise. Would you do that for an old man?"

The reverend looked so pitiful that his request would have melted the coldest of hearts. The young men followed him home caravan-style, the pastors driving their late model autos, Reverend Dean leading the way with his sixteen-year-old Ford. Pastor Taylik, bringing up the rear, didn't know whether to blame John Snead or Reverend Dean for their dismal, thirty-mile-an-hour pace. He ultimately blamed both of them. Finally, after fifteen minutes, the convoy arrived at 51 Bunyan Ave.

As they entered the living room, Reverend Dean collected his guests' coats and laid them carefully on the bed in his bedroom. "Please," he gestured, returning to the main room, "be seated. I'll make us some fresh coffee."

Several minutes later, preceded by the smell of ground beans and a gurgling coffeemaker, the reverend returned with three mugs of steaming French Roast.

Upon taking a sip, John Snead rubbed his fingers and thumb together for several seconds. Noticing his host's quizzical expression, he felt obliged to explain. "I'm sorry, Thaddeus, this mug's rather, ah . . . sticky," he smiled apologetically.

"I'm afraid mine is, as well," Rick Taylik echoed.

"My friends, I am so sorry! I must have spilled some sugar on the outside of the mugs! This is so embarrassing! I would replace them, but the rest are in the dishwasher!"

The old man blushed a deep red. If she were alive, Emma would have been horrified.

"But, I assure you, the insides are quite clean. Here you are doing me a favor, and I repay you by serving you with sticky mugs!"

The young men had to smile, and the conversation quickly turned to various innocuous topics. Finally, the ice broken, the subject turned to that morning's events.

"Thaddeus," Rick Taylik ventured, "what do you make of all this? I mean, the two visitors coming, and Steve dying after their ... proclamations. Could this really be *supernatural* in origin?"

"God can do anything, Rick," the reverend replied evenly, "but before I come down one way or the other, I'd like to see the autopsy report."

"But, Reverend, you're relying on facts, and our purview is faith!" John Snead responded. "It's well and good to suggest logic and rigid analysis, but surely we, as Christians, know of something better."

"With all candor, my friend," the old man countered, "I couldn't disagree with you more. I've long thought that if a belief system isn't logical, then no amount of faith is going to make it palatable. Only if the *basics* are rational, will I commit to believing — through faith — the parts I don't understand. But surely you agree," he asked, extending a hand to invite reply.

The silence surprised him. However, since no one changed the subject, he decided to proceed.

"For example, it strains credulity past the breaking point, does it not, to believe that human life was created purely by chance? The odds — trillions and trillions to one — are simply too great.[7] Consequently, I believe that logic points toward a creator."

The old man paused. He had no desire to bore his new friends.

Hearing no rebuttal, however, he continued.

"Similarly, it defies reason that a creator would make a world and simply walk away from it. Thus, in my opinion, it's logical that He would communicate with us. And — in fact — various creeds assert He did. How then do we decide which is correct?

"All major religions — with one exception — agree on one point: that people are basically good, and that if we try hard enough, we can work our way to what some call heaven, nirvana or enlightenment.

"The sole exception is Christianity. It stands apart from other religions in its central tenet: that man *can't* work his way to heaven, because he isn't — and can never be — good enough."

The old man paused for a reply. None was forthcoming. He couldn't tell if this was due to his eloquence, or because his guests were offended. He decided to come quickly to his point.

"But surely a belief which tells man that he's good is deluding itself. Even if we limit ourselves to examples during my lifetime, we still have the Holocaust, Stalin's gulags, Mao's Cultural Revolution, Pol Pot's killing fields, and the massacre of the Tutus in Rwanda. Perhaps it highlights my point that, in order to keep this list short, I've had to limit it to deaths of one million or more."

The old man paused, contemplating evil on such a massive scale.

"Thus, I do not dismiss logic because I have faith. Rather — due to its unique view of man — logic leads me *to* my faith."

An awkward silence enveloped the reverend's living room. Pastor Snead stared at his coffee, while Rick Taylik gazed out the window.

"Ahh, my friends . . . I have lapsed into that lamentable, but all too common, foible of retired pastors: preaching to those who have not come for a sermon."

The pudgy man extended his arms in repentance.

"Please. Accept my apology."

"Actually, Reverend, rather than resenting your thoughts, I was pondering them," said the music director, smoothing his pants as he rose. "However, together with what's happened this morning, I don't think I can absorb any more. Reverend Dean, thank you for your hospitality, and for a thought-provoking discussion. But I'm sure you'll understand my need to reflect on all that's happened today."

"I, too, want to thank you, Reverend," said Rick Taylik. "This has been very interesting. I only wish you would bring this kind of analysis to Steve's death."

To their surprise, both men saw an unusual gleam in Reverend Dean's eyes; a glint which suggested he might be more than a retiree who served coffee in sticky mugs.

In fact, both guests became slightly uncomfortable.

"With the Lord's help, this logic *will* be brought to my friend's death," the reverend declared. "You can be . . . *very* . . . sure of that."

Chapter 3

Puppadawg was just about to take Reverend Dean for a walk when they were interrupted by the telephone. The massive St. Bernard huffed in annoyance, dropped his leash, and padded to the living room.

"Thaddeus Dean."

"Reverend, this is Rick Taylik. I thought you might like an update on Steve's death."

It was Wednesday, three days after his friend's passing. He would like nothing better.

"Of course, Rick. Please go ahead."

"He was *poisoned*, Reverend. And they also found poison in the remnants of his communion cup!"

"Just in . . . *Steve's* cup?"

"That's right. No one else's." The young man fought to control his bewilderment. "But how could that *be*? I mean, the tray was full of cups, all filled with juice. How could anyone know which cup he'd choose? Unless. . ."

"Yes, Rick?"

"Reverend, there is *one* person who would know. I mean . . . *God* would know. Reverend, do you . . . do you think there might be something supernatural to this, after all?"

Reverend Dean chose not to answer.

"Rick, who filled the communion cups with juice last Sunday?"

Taylik took a moment to compose himself. "Well, ordinarily it would have been my turn, but I was running late with the coffee, so I asked Pastor Snead to do it for me. So, as far as I know, John filled the cups last Sunday."

The anxious pastor paused, but not for long.

"But what *difference* does that make, Reverend? There was no way for John — or anyone else — to know which cup Steve would choose. It was one of over thirty cups in the tray."

The young man lowered his voice, but sounded all the more intense for doing so.

"Reverend," he said solemnly, "if God didn't do it, *then it doesn't make any logical sense.*"

"Oh, it makes perfect sense," the reverend replied. "It makes perfect, horrible sense."

"What . . . what do you mean?"

"Are you busy tonight?" Reverend Dean inquired.

"Not if you need me."

"Fine. Come over around seven o'clock, and be sure to bring Pastor Snead with you. Will you do that?"

"We'll be there."

Reverend Dean sighed. First Christmas, and now this.

It wasn't that he didn't enjoy the holidays. It was merely that, without Emma, they were a lonely affair. The first Christmas after her death, he made the mistake of decorating their Christmas tree by himself. Afterwards, he became terribly depressed. Puppadawg, sensing something was wrong, stood by his side throughout the day. After that, he made a point to invite someone over whenever he decorated his small house.

This year, however, he hadn't even started; and Christmas was just two weeks away. He tried to tell himself that he'd simply forgotten, but he knew the real reason: no matter who kept him company, it just wasn't the same.

And now this. The death of one of his closest friends.

The duel blows, however, didn't affect the old man's mind. He knew who had murdered his friend, and how it was done. Indeed, that was the easy part. The hard part would be convincing this man to spare his church the shame and publicity of a trial.

He shook his head. He wasn't optimistic about those chances.

As he debated what to say, a cold, wet nose nudged him above the beltline. Most dogs nuzzled their owner's knees. A few, their thighs. Puppadawg had no trouble poking the squat reverend in the side.

"Are you still in the mood to go outside?" the old man asked. "How about a drive to the bookstore? They have live reindeer outside. Would you like to see them? Eh?"

Reverend Dean's favorite store, exceeding even Starbucks, was Dark Pine's bookstore. The fact that they were next to each other made the location irresistible. Whenever he had been late for dinner, Emma always knew exactly where to call to prod him home.

Each year, primarily as a treat for children, the bookstore arranged for a pair of reindeer to live in a makeshift barn outside the store. The reindeer always brought a smile to his face, and he desperately needed something to lift his spirits. Puppadawg, sensing a trip, barked in approval.

Two hours later, the old man returned home. The reindeer were charming, the bookstore delightful and Puppadawg content.

But there were still no decorations in his home.

And he still had no idea how to appeal to a murderer's sense of duty.

Chapter 4

At 6:55 a car pulled into the reverend's driveway. Reverend Dean opened his door to Rick Taylik and John Snead before they could ring the doorbell.

"Gentlemen, I'm glad you arrived. Please, come in."

Pastor Snead, stylish as ever, was miffed.

"Reverend, Rick said you had some insight into Steve's death, so of course I came. But couldn't we have done this over the phone?"

"Not as satisfactorily, no," he replied cryptically. "Please, sit down."

Unlike last Sunday, Reverend Dean didn't wear a suit. Nonetheless, perhaps due to the change in his demeanor, his worn slacks and faded shirt commanded more respect than his former attire.

At least it seemed that way to his visitors.

"I'll be blunt," the reverend began. "This meeting is an attempt to convince the murderer of Steve Ragsdale to clear his conscience, and repent of his crime."

The jaws of both men dropped.

Immediately before their protests began.

"Reverend, really. . ."

"I can't *believe* you would—"

"*Stop*," commanded the old man with surprising firmness. "I see I'm not being taken seriously. Very well. Allow me to convince you that I know what happened."

The short, portly cleric walked behind a chair and grabbed its tattered backrest with his stubby fingers.

"I can only guess at the motive, but I imagine it was one of the oldest: naked ambition, perhaps mixed with a dollop of theological disgust. Steve Ragsdale was just a middle-aged man, with many good years ahead of him. If either of you wished to stay in Dark Pine, you had to resign yourself to playing second-fiddle for at least a couple of decades. Even that might have been palatable, if Steve had agreed with your theology. But in your denomination, Steve's evangelical beliefs chafed like a stone in a shoe. Two decades as a subordinate was bad enough. Two decades as the subordinate of someone you didn't respect was intolerable.

"But how to get rid of such a man?" The reverend gazed at the ceiling, as if he were the killer, contemplating his crime. "The most logical method wouldn't just involve killing Steve, but murdering him in a way that defamed him; and implicated someone else."

The reverend looked at both pastors with sadness.

"This was done with a skill worthy of the vilest criminal. From a man trusted by Steve; worse, by a man supposedly devoted to our Lord."

The reverend shook his head, then continued.

"The plan was brilliant, in an evil kind of way," he admitted. "Who better to impugn a pastor than God?

"So the murderer hired two actors. One, a tall ex-athlete, with dazzling blond hair and an imposing physique. The other, a man picked to match our notion of what Jesus looked like. Their mission was to appear in church, point an accusing finger at a pastor, and recite three verses of Scripture. That's all. Not very hard work. In fact, I'm sure the murderer had no trouble at all importing actors to perform this stunt. They were probably told it was some sort of joke. They had no clue it was a prelude to murder."

The reverend sat in a chair, placed an elbow on each armrest, and steepled his fingers. Grimly, he looked at the men in front of him.

"But *we* know, don't we?" he asked softly. Neither visitor spoke.

"Once the idea — the despicable idea — that Steve harbored some secret sin was planted, the second half of this plan could proceed. The actual murder."

"*Reverend*," Taylik interrupted, "I not only resent your accusations, but we've already been through this. There was no way anyone could predict which cup Steve would select."

"You're right."

The reverend paused, then tilted his head toward his questioner.

"That's why you poisoned him beforehand."

"How *dare* you!" spat Taylik. "Not only have you slandered me, but you've done it in front of a witness. I'll take everything you've got, you stupid old man, and see you thrown out on the street."

Although Pastor Snead was stunned by his friend's outburst, Reverend Dean took it in stride.

"That might be difficult to do," he suggested, "if you're in prison."

"Fine. I'll hear this out," he said venomously. "If only to get more ammunition for my slander suit. *When* was I supposed to have poisoned Steve? And why was there poison in his communion cup, if that's not what killed him?"

"I said that you were a murderer, Rick; not that you were

stupid," the old man said calmly. "To answer your questions, you poisoned him before the service, when you handed him his coffee. You were in charge of the coffee service that morning. It would have been a simple matter to coat the inside of a cup with poison, and then — when Steve approached the table — pull that cup out and pour his coffee in the tainted mug."

"There's no way you can prove that."

The reverend met Taylik's glare with a determined gaze of his own. Ignoring the comment, he continued.

"The trick, of course, was to make people think that the poison came from somewhere else. If the police believed that Steve was poisoned before church began, they would immediately examine the person who served him coffee. So you gave them another option. You arranged for visits by an 'angel' and 'Jesus' to make people think that Steve wouldn't be harmed before Communion."

"But one of them *vanished*!" Snead objected, finally speaking. "The entire church saw it happen!"

"With all due respect, John, no one saw anything of the sort. All you saw was 'Jesus' walk into the pastors' study, with Rick in hot pursuit. Shortly thereafter, Rick emerged and informed you that the man had vanished."

"Well, then . . . what *did* happen? How did he vanish?"

"Oh, that's simple enough," the reverend explained. "Rick lied. He made sure that he was the first person to pursue 'Jesus,' to forestall anyone else who had the same idea. Once the actor entered the study, he 'vanished' the way most people leave a room. He walked out the door. Rick had unlocked the exterior door before church began, and relocked the door as soon as the actor left the study. It would have taken mere seconds. Even if someone followed Rick, they would have been too late to see 'Jesus.' And if someone tried to *accompany* Rick, I'm sure he would have told them to wait outside the study. And there's little doubt they would have obeyed. Few parishioners would challenge a pastor in front of his congregation."

"You haven't answered *my* question," sneered Taylik.

"My apologies," the reverend replied, with no sincerity. "Where was I?" The cleric briefly furrowed his brow.

"Ah, yes. Your plan to point the police to the communion cup, and away from the coffee cup. To continue, then. After your actors planted the idea of Steve's 'unworthiness' in people's minds, you made sure that *you* were sitting at the end of the pastors' pew last Sunday morning. This was critical, because after Steve drank from the communion cup, you would be the one to take the tray of used cups and place it inside the podium.

"After you noted which cup Steve had used, you sprinkled a powdered form of the poison into that empty cup. A liquid form would have been possible, but that would have required a vial and cap, which would have been difficult to manipulate with one hand."

"I suppose you think that's relevant, you stupid old fool."

The reverend paused. A smile almost crossed his lips.

"In any event," he continued, "Poisoning the correct cup was necessary in the unlikely event that the police used DNA testing to determine which cup Steve drank from. Fortunately for you, it wasn't hard to keep track of Steve's cup, because there were only three people using that tray. Afterwards, you made sure the tray was preserved, so the police could analyze it and discover the poison. They would never suspect that someone would put poison in a cup *after* it had been used. Of course, before all this happened, you made sure that John was the person who filled the communion cups."

The reverend turned toward his second, and increasingly shocked, guest.

"As you may recall, John, in order to get you to fill the

communion cups, Rick gave the excuse that he was busy with the coffee that morning. In that regard, at least, he was telling the truth."

"Rick! Is this true? Did you do such a thing?"

By now the accused pastor had regained his composure. "Of course not, John," he smoothly reassured his friend. "Tragically, Reverend Dean is showing his age, and he's fixated on the slanderous idea of me as a murderer. But you've known me for years. Do *you* think I could do such a thing?"

"Well, it is rather outlandish. . ."

"I agree," said Reverend Dean. "That's why I said nothing until Rick told me the results of the police toxicology report. By the way, Rick, you never mentioned which poison was used."

"How should *I* know!" the pastor bellowed.

"Ah. Thank you. I wanted to confirm in front of a witness that I had no idea which poison was involved."

"What difference does *that* make?" Taylik roared. He was starting to lose his composure again.

"I'm sorry, I keep forgetting. It has to do with the proof, of course."

Taylik abruptly closed his mouth.

"Steve Ragsdale had been a very close friend for many years," the reverend explained. "And his death was certainly a shock. But immediately after his death, did you really think I needed to be with the only men who could have killed him, merely to conduct an impromptu wake?"

Neither guest ventured a response.

"Nor am I so senile," explained Thaddeus Dean, "that I would serve sticky mugs to guests without cause. In this case, the reason was to collect any traces of powdered poison from the murderer's fingers before he could wash them off."

"But . . . but," Snead sputtered, "that's *absurd*. How would you know which hand or fingers the poison was on? And how would you know it would stick to a mug? I mean, this is too much."

"You're right, John. The mugs were a long shot. But at the time I didn't know which of you had killed Steve. And since only one of you wore gloves, I had to improvise. There was no other way to collect a sample from both of you."

"I . . . I don't understand," Snead blurted. "*Gloves*?"

Reverend Dean cocked an eyebrow. "Did I forget that? I must be 'showing my age' again, as Rick put it. I wrapped a cotton swab in double-sided tape, and inserted it into each finger of the gloves which I laid with your coats in my bedroom. It would provide a decent sample of poisonous powder, if any was present. As you may recall, John, you didn't wear gloves last Sunday. Thus, I was able to devote my entire attention to the gloves which Rick wore. I later gave the tape and mugs to the police, and they made some interesting findings."

Reverend Dean turned to Rick Taylik. Judging from the pastor's murderous expression, if Snead hadn't been present the reverend would have been his next victim.

"And *that* explains," the reverend clarified, "why I needed to confirm that you hadn't told me — when you summarized the police report over the phone — which poison was used. Now you can't claim that I knew which poison to put on the samples I gave the police, in some misguided effort to frame you."

As Reverend Dean finished, a red light began to pulsate outside the living room window.

"That would be Detective Small," the reverend explained quietly. His expression toward Taylik softened. Slightly.

"Dark Pine is a small town. It will be a simple matter to track down the actors from the few hotel registries. I fear that is bad news for you, Rick. In any event, I was sincere in what I said earlier this evening. I urge you to confess your crime, and spare your church the embarrassment of a trial. It's not too late to think of your flock."

The reverend paused. "Rick, it's not too late to repent."

"Save it, you senile old toad," spat Taylik. "It was just luck that got you this far, and it'll take more than that to send me to prison."

Both men rose at the sound of the doorbell. On his way to the door, the reverend paused in front of the livid pastor.

"Luck had nothing to do with it, Rick. Don't you remember our discussion last Sunday? I promised that logic would be brought to bear on Steve's murder. And so it was. Guided by my Lord, it was logic that allowed me to see how you committed this terrible act."

The reverend paused, and lowered his voice before opening the door.

"And it's logic that tells me it will be many, many years before you darken the streets of this town again."

Chapter 5

The following weekend the sky was powder blue, the exact shade his friend would have liked. Steve Ragsdale appreciated sunny days as much as Reverend Dean enjoyed rainy ones. The reverend had taken Puppadawg to the cemetery but, atypically, had unhooked his companion's leash and allowed the dog to run amidst the tombstones. He needed to be alone; even from his four-legged friend.

The old man looked despondently at the headstone.

"I have been so busy bringing justice to your memory that I haven't had a chance to mourn you," he whispered. "I miss you tremendously my friend. I—"

He tried to say more, but his sobs held him back.

Murder in a Sealed Loft

Chapter 1

The two of them were quietly gathered in Reverend Dean's basement den. The guest — at twenty-six, the youngest of Dark Pine's two police detectives — stared at a smoldering fireplace from the vantage of a worn recliner. The host, knowing his friend would eventually speak, watched two doves nibble at seed he'd poured in a feeder earlier that day.

Reverend Dean had known Detective Mark Small his entire life. He'd babysat him as an infant, baptized him as a boy, and watched him develop as a policeman. Because the reverend had no children, Mark was the closest thing he had to a son. He loved him dearly, and the young man reciprocated; particularly after his father — the reverend's best friend — passed away several years ago.

Mark was unmarried, but it wasn't because his girlfriend hadn't dropped several hints. Reverend Dean understood the appeal. Mark's curly brown hair, freckled face, and gangly good looks would attract almost any girl. Unfortunately, Mark took his time when making decisions. He usually arrived at the correct result, but the wait could be lengthy. Take this afternoon, for example.

Mark hadn't said a word for five minutes.

The reverend slouched on the sofa. He'd contracted a severe case of flu, and was very tired. In fact, he hadn't been this sick in years. The fact that Mark would risk the reverend's flu meant the young man was deeply troubled. Two minutes later, the detective sighed, took a deep breath and finally began.

"I'm sorry to bother you when you're sick, Reverend. But I've got a very peculiar case and I don't know what I'm missing."

The young man paused. "Actually, I *do* know what I'm missing: *who* did it, *how* he did it and *why* he did it." He turned and smiled. "Have I left anything out?"

"There's nothing like a puzzle to take the mind off one's infirmities," the old man graciously allowed. "And in any event, at least you know *where* it was done and *what* was done. That's two-fifths of the equation, isn't it? Who, what, where, why and how?" he gently suggested.

"I suppose. For all the good it does me. Do you know how embarrassing it is when you can't explain how a murder occurred? That's for mystery novels, Reverend, not real life. The captain is annoyed."

"I only know what I've read in the papers. Why don't you go over it for me?"

The detective shrugged with obvious pessimism.

"That's why I'm here, I suppose." He slowly pulled the footrest into the recliner and sat on the edge of the chair. "Okay, here's what happened.

"Dan and Marie Jennings had been married for fourteen years. Neither had been married previously. Dan managed a furniture store, while Marie painted. She was apparently pretty good — even sold a few paintings. Still, most of their money was from Dan's salary."

"A happy marriage?" inquired the reverend with a cough.

"So-so. Apparently they had their ups and downs, but no one heard them mention divorce. Anyway, Marie rented a nearby apartment to use as a studio. There are four apartments in that building, two upstairs and two downstairs. She had an upstairs unit.

"Last Saturday, Marie left home at approximately 9:00 AM to paint in her studio. We know she arrived shortly thereafter, because she placed an "800" call from her apartment to an artist supply store at 9:10. At approximately 9:30, her husband drove to the apartment with Jeff Astor, the assistant manager of Dan's store. They were met there by Randy Goodloe, who lives in a house next to the apartment building. Randy and Jeff had volunteered to help Dan mow the grass, do some painting, and various other maintenance chores."

"That's unusual, isn't it? I mean, none of them owns the building."

"That's true. But apparently Dan and Marie are friends with the owner — an elderly woman named Margaret Flakely — and Dan agreed to perform maintenance work in exchange for a rent reduction. And Dan's friends have been helping each other with yard work for years.

"Anyway, after they finished their work around 1:00 in the afternoon, all three men went up to the apartment to have a cold drink."

"Had anyone been in the apartment earlier that day?"

"No. In fact, Jeff Astor and Randy Goodloe had never been in the apartment — Marie called it her loft — and Dan hadn't been inside for weeks."

Mark stood and began to pace.

"Here's where it gets confusing. The men knock on the door for several minutes. Marie doesn't answer. They know she's inside because her car is parked nearby. They knock so loudly that neighbors open their doors to see what's going on. There's still no answer. Finally Dan becomes worried and decides to break the door down. It takes them a while to do this because Marie has three locks on the door, but they finally get in. They find Marie, dead on the floor, stabbed through the heart."

"Good heavens," the old man murmured. The paper had reported most of the details, but it was shocking, nonetheless.

"Didn't Dan have a key to the apartment?"

"Yes, but only to one lock. The other two could only be locked from the inside."

"Windows?"

"Several, all locked."

The old man stroked his chin in thought, which prompted another cough. "What did the men do next?"

"Well, Dan took a few steps inside and immediately knelt next to his wife. He was understandably distraught. Jeff tried to dial 911, but the kitchen phone didn't work. No one knew if the murderer was still there, so Jeff asked Randy to come with him as he searched for another phone; a logical request, since Randy is six foot five and two hundred sixty pounds. They called from another room, searched the apartment, but found no one. Afterwards, they rejoined Dan in the living room. We arrived fifteen minutes later. When—"

"Wait. Did anything happen between the phone call and your arrival?"

"Well, no. I mean, she was already dead, so there was nothing anyone could do."

The young man paused and thought for several seconds.

"Wait a minute, there was one thing. Apparently Marie had brought their German Shepherd to the loft with her. It growled something fierce at Randy; acted like it had a grudge against him. Anyway, it became so bad that Dan had to shut the dog in the bedroom."

The old man looked for a box of tissue paper, found the carton and pulled out several tissues. "I'm not clear on the layout of the apartment, or where the body was found."

"Their apartment has a living room, kitchen, dining area, one bathroom and two bedrooms. As you step into the apartment, the dining area is on the left, and the living room is on the right. Marie was found in the area between the two rooms, just as you enter the apartment. As you walk further into the unit, you pass the kitchen on your left, one bedroom on your right, the bathroom further down on your left and the second bedroom — the largest — at the end of the hallway. Marie used this room as her studio."

"Furnishings?" asked the reverend, blowing his nose in the tissues.

"Typical artist studio paraphernalia: paint, paintbrushes, framed canvas on easels and tarps to protect the floor. The first bedroom had a cot for naps, a chair, a filing cabinet and a desk used for paperwork. The living room had the bare essentials: an old sofa, a coffee table and a padded chair. The kitchen had a table and two folding chairs."

"Any dirty dishes?"

"No. Everything had been washed."

"Ashtrays?"

"None. She didn't smoke."

"Could the windows have been opened from the outside?"

"No. And keep in mind, three men were working outside the whole time. How could anyone enter or leave without being seen?"

The old man began to answer, thought better of it, then tossed the tissues into a wastebasket.

"Tell me about the body," he asked instead.

"Marie Jennings was laid out parallel to the door, her head in the living room and her feet in the dining area. She was found on her back, with a knife sticking out of her at a forty-five degree angle. The handle pointed toward her feet, with the blade sliding under her ribs into her heart."

"Blood?"

"Copious amounts on, under and around the body. It's clear that she was stabbed in that area."

The pastor rose and walked slowly to the window. He was almost too tired to stand, but he suffered from Restless Leg Syndrome, a disorder which only subsided when he stood.[8] The doves had abandoned the birdfeeder. Empty, it swayed gently in the wind. It seemed almost lonely. Or perhaps that's just how he felt, ever since Emma died. He shook his head and returned to the topic.

"So Dan and Jeff arrived together, and Randy met them there?" inquired the reverend, still looking at the feeder.

"More or less. Jeff followed Dan in his truck. But Randy did meet them there. He lives virtually next door."

"But he's never been in the loft?"

"That's what he says."

"I suppose suicide has been ruled out?"

"Yes. Even if Marie pulled the blade into herself, there were no prints on the handle, and no nearby cloth to explain a lack of prints. Also, for what it's worth, she was murdered close to the time her body was found."

"So," the old man recapped, "we have what appears to be an impossible crime. Someone stabbed this unfortunate woman, yet the murder was performed while she was behind a door with three locks — two of which could only be locked from the inside —

windows which were locked, and a large dog guarding the interior."

The detective sunk his head in his hands. "That's right," he mumbled.

"Worse," he continued to the detective's annoyance, "the murder occurred while three witnesses were working around the building, thus insuring that no one could leave the unit unnoticed."

Mark raised his head and sighed.

"Actually, it's even worse than that. Assuming the killer might be hiding in another apartment, we searched the other three units — much to the annoyance of the old ladies who live there — and found nothing. However, we did establish that none of them had ever visited Marie. Nor had any other friends, for that matter.

"Then we thought her killer might have hid under the stairwell while the men broke in Marie's unit, then slipped out while they were in her apartment. That didn't happen either. The building's back door was locked, and a tenant had been sitting on a porch near the front door for over twenty minutes before the men went upstairs. She saw no one leave; although she *did* say this was the most excitement she'd had in years.

"And in case you were wondering, we searched all three men, as well as Dan's car and Jeff's truck. There was nothing incriminating on the men or in their vehicles. We also searched the apartment with a fine-tooth comb. We found nothing out of place, with one possible exception. According to Dan, two paperweights and a stapler were missing from Marie's desk. But we have no idea if they were taken by the killer, or simply discarded by Marie during the last few weeks."

"Now that's interesting," the pastor began, his eyes brightening, "because—"

The reverend was interrupted by a series of beeps from Mark's pager. The detective raised the device and squinted at its readout. "Got to go," the young man said, striding to the door. "I'll call tonight, and you can finish your thought."

Reverend Dean sat in the darkening room and wheezed. Unlike his puzzled friend, he saw no problem with how the murder might have been committed. He knew at least four ways someone could accomplish it.

However, there were some intriguing anomalies.

The missing items, for one thing. And the dog. And finally, the knife angle. Unfortunately they raised more questions than they answered. He shook his head and walked slowly up the stairs. Frequently it was best to let problems percolate. Particularly since he didn't know the people involved, and was too sick to visit the scene. If he was going to help, any suggestions would come solely from what Mark told him. The reverend smiled and sneezed at the same time. He hoped his friend had other leads. If a housebound retiree was his only source of help, he was in more trouble than he knew.

Reaching the top of the stairs, he shuffled into his deserted kitchen. It was still difficult, three years after his wife's death, to imagine living without Emma. Like most couples of their generation, Emma had done most of the cooking. He smiled when he recalled how she hummed when she prepared a new dinner. She knew it pleased him to try new dishes, and — like the best of marriages — that meant it pleased her as well. And whenever Emma was happy, she hummed.

What would she have made tonight, he wondered?

Reverend Dean's nose began to tingle. That always happened when he thought of Emma. He knew that if he didn't think of something else, his eyes would start to tear. He focused on dinner. He spied a box of Hamburger Helper that he'd bought on sale at

Wal-Mart. It looked good and it wouldn't hurt his sore throat. He pulled out a skillet and turned on the burner.

As the mixture simmered away, he opened a can of Puppadawg's favorite food. Long ago, Reverend Dean had learned that if the St. Bernard didn't have his own food at supper time, he felt entitled to share whatever his owner was having. Emma took a dim view of that, so for over a decade their meals had been coordinated. The old man couldn't remember the last time he'd had dinner without Puppadawg at his feet, slobbering away in his gigantic dish.

If the weather wasn't bad, the pair usually took a walk afterwards. If the reverend forgot, Puppadawg stood at the door with such sad eyes that the cleric quickly remembered. Tonight, due to his flu, the reverend took a nap instead. He awoke to the sound of a ringing phone.

"Curiouser and curiouser," Mark blurted, forgoing introduction. "Am I interrupting anything?"

"Not at all," the old man graciously replied. In fact, he'd been hoping Mark would call.

"The medical examiner confirmed that Marie was, in fact, killed around the time the men found her."

"*But. . .*" guessed the cleric, interpreting Mark's tone perfectly.

"But," admitted the detective, "half the blood around her contained red blood cells that had burst."

The pastor didn't know what to do with this information.

"I don't understand. Was it *her* blood?"

"Oh yes. DNA confirms that every drop of blood came from the deceased."

"Then . . . what does that mean? What would cause ruptured blood cells?"

"Per the M.E., several things. But he's betting on extreme cold. He thinks the blood was frozen."

"*All* of it?"

"No. Just half. But get this. He swears the body wasn't frozen — ever."

"That is . . . the oddest thing I've ever heard," confessed the reverend, perplexed by this development.

"Are you ready for the second half of the report?"

He covered the phone with his hand and coughed. "I suppose."

"The frozen blood also showed traces of anti-coagulants."

"Which means . . . what? That she'd recently had surgery?"

"Actually, she *did* have elective surgery last month," Mark conceded with admiration. "But it wasn't that kind of anticoagulant. The usual anticoagulant you get in surgery is heparin. That's used, for example, during heart bypass operations. But the anticoagulant found in half of Marie Jennings' blood was CPDA; a combination of citrate, phosphate, dextrose and adenine."

"Well, I'm no doctor," the pastor said, stating the obvious. "What did the M.E. infer from the anticoagulants?"

"He thinks the blood was donated. According to him, all blood given at a blood bank has anticoagulants in the bag where the blood is stored; otherwise it immediately begins to clot. So the question is: why would a woman — murdered at approximately 1:00 PM on a Saturday afternoon — be covered with blood that she'd previously donated?"

Neither man had an answer.

"I think," suggested the portly reverend, "that I should take a walk with Puppadawg and give this some thought. Perhaps I'll be up to it tomorrow."

Mark was unimpressed.

"Humph," he grunted. "Well, call me as soon as Puppadawg gives you the answer. Because at this point I don't know any more than he does."

* * *

The following afternoon the reverend felt no better, so instead of taking Puppadawg for a walk he kept the great beast in the back yard. Puppadawg was disappointed, but accepted his fate with nothing more than a snort.

Although Reverend Dean enjoyed their strolls as much as Puppadawg, he consoled himself by indulging in one of his favorite activities: a steam bath. Early in their marriage, Emma had learned — with some dismay — that the reverend enjoyed turning their shower to "hot," shutting the bathroom door, and reading cross-legged next to the shower in the misty bathroom. It was the reverend's makeshift "steam room," and even though the water heater quickly emptied, he enjoyed the atmosphere while it lasted.

Although Emma was more longsuffering than most wives — a pastor's wife has to be — she took a dim view of the empty water heater and peeling paint that resulted from the steam. Consequently, when she suggested they build a second bathroom, complete with a steam shower, the reverend was only slightly more enthusiastic than she was. Two years later, they had saved enough money for their tiny new bathroom. Two members of the church — a carpenter and a plumber — helped build the addition, and the reverend had joyously used the steam shower ever since.

What he never found out was that Emma had cleaned houses for months to save money for the steam machine. She kept it a secret because she knew her husband would never agree to a steamer if it meant a sacrifice by his wife. But if Emma had known how happy it would make her husband, she would have made the sacrifice long ago.

Now the only damage from the reverend's hobby was the condition of the paperbacks in his library. He couldn't bring any valuable or borrowed books in the steam bath because it ruined the paper. So — unless he went in the steam bath solely to pray — he selected one of his paperbacks to accompany him. What entered the steamer as a normal-sized book emerged forty minutes later as a swollen monstrosity three times its prior size. After it dried, the reverend wedged the engorged volume back into a bookcase. Until it dried, however, visitors would witness the peculiar sight of several damp, bloated paperbacks, arrayed in a row on his study floor, in various stages of dampness.

The reverend stepped in the shower, closed the door and turned on the steamer. As it hissed and began to heat the water, he pushed a cheap, plastic lawn chair into the stall corner and slowly lowered himself into the chair. The old man watched the steam condense into beads on the opaque door, swell into large drops, and scurry down the drain. He took halting, deep breaths. He imagined the enveloping steam was medicine, soothing his lungs and healing his flu. It was several minutes before he turned to Mark's problem.

He had quickly realized, of course, how it might have been accomplished. That wasn't the problem.

The problem wasn't even the paperweights.

The problem was the stapler.

The unfortunate victim might have thrown away a pair of paperweights. Reverend Dean had seen a good many ugly ones during his lifetime, and most people didn't even use them; opting instead for anything nearby in the few instances when they were truly needed. So much for the paperweights, then.

But people didn't usually throw away staplers. Virtually all home offices had them. So perhaps the paperweights and the stapler were linked. But how?

And what about the dog's strange behavior?

Annoyed at his inability to see a pattern, Reverend Dean cleared him mind and began to pray. He usually grouped his prayers into several categories: first praise, then thanks, followed by asking forgiveness, then seeking God's help. Unlike some

Christians, however, he added a fifth category: silently waiting for any answers the Holy Spirit might give. Not with an audible voice, of course, but by gentle suggestions to his consciousness. In this hectic age, many Christians ignored this aspect of prayer. The old man viewed this with sadness. Why ask, if you don't wait for a response? Granted, answers didn't always come, but — more often than not — something did. Oddly enough, the answers he usually received were to questions he *hadn't* asked.

After fifty minutes, the reverend struggled up from the chair. As he turned on the main shower to rinse himself, he realized that no answers — to the murder at least — would come tonight.

Chapter 2

Thaddeus Dean, long of the opinion that early risers had a personality defect, was not particularly charitable when his phone rang at 9:00 the following morning. Combined with his flu — which showed no signs of abating — the old man was positively cranky.

As usual, Mark dispensed with opening pleasantries.

"I've got it. I've solved the case."

"Indeed," mumbled the reverend, stumbling from his bed to the coffeemaker in the kitchen.

"The chief is quite pleased. I make the arrest this afternoon."

"Mark, I need to put you down for a minute."

Without waiting for a reply, the pastor dropped the phone on the counter and shoveled far more coffee than was recommended into his coffeemaker. He filled the machine with water and placed his mug where the coffeepot usually sat. As the brown drops filled his cup, he gave a satisfied grunt and retrieved the phone.

"Now then. Where were we?"

Mark was annoyed that his breakthrough had been met with such restraint. "Well, we *were* discussing how I solved the case," he huffed, "but if you want, I can call back after I've made the arrest."

"Now, now. Don't get upset just because I need caffeine to keep up with you," reassured the old man. "So tell me how you've solved the case."

"It was a classic example of misdirection," the detective gloated. "And pretty smart, too, I must admit. It was the husband, of course."

Reverend Dean examined his mug and decided he couldn't wait for more than half a cup. He balanced the phone on his shoulder, switched the mug with the coffee pot, and poured powdered milk and sugar into his coffee.

"Perhaps you'd better start at the beginning."

"I know, I know. I'm excited," the young man admitted. He calmed himself with a deep breath and started over. "Okay. Let's return to that Saturday morning. The wife enters her loft around nine, right?"

"So we're told."

"And that's just what *did* happen. That much is true. Then things start to get weird. Dan Jennings comes to the apartment right after his wife makes her phone call—"

"Can you prove that?"

"Not yet. But that's the only way he could have managed it. I questioned the men again, and when they were working there was never a time when either Goodloe or Astor didn't have visual contact with the husband. In other words, there was never a time when the husband was alone while the men were cleaning the yard. And since *only* the husband could have killed his wife, he must have entered the loft before the yard work started."

The detective paused, then mumbled, "Otherwise this really *is* impossible."

"Go on," the pastor said noncommittally, savoring his first sip of coffee.

"So the husband shows up after his wife makes the phone call, and knocks her unconscious. Then—"

"I hate to interrupt, but I assume the M.E. found a bruise to support this theory?"

"Not yet, Reverend, but *listen*."

"Okay, okay," he reassured his friend.

"So the husband goes home, returns with Astor a few minutes later, works in the yard, and enters the apartment at 1:00 with his friends. What do they see? What they assume is a dead woman. Only she's *not* dead. She's just unconscious."

"So where did the blood come from?"

"That's the beauty of it. Dan Jennings knows there has to be blood on his wife, and he knows we can tell if it's *her* blood or not. He also knows we can tell the difference between fresh blood and blood that's been drying for three hours. So he gets a pint of his wife's blood, *freezes it*, and simply places the frozen block of blood on top of his unconscious wife. By the time they enter the apartment at 1:00, it's melted and it will pass as fresh blood — or so he thinks."

"And the knife sticking out of the woman?"

"Again, I've got to give the husband credit. It's a real knife handle, *but without a blade*. It's meant to deceive the friends into thinking that she'd been stabbed. He taped it to her after knocking her unconscious."

"Well, I suppose, but—"

"It all fits, Reverend. Remember what the friends did when they entered the apartment with the husband? They *left the room* to call 911, and then they searched the rest of the loft. That gave the husband the time he needed. He pocketed the handle, took a *real* knife from his pocket, and pushed it into his unconscious — but soon to be dead — wife. When his friends came back in the room, the deed had been done. Slick, no?"

Reverend Dean drained his mug and poured himself a full cup.

Finally, his mind began to stir.

"Slick, yes. But why did Dan go through all this trouble? Why not kill Marie in a less conspicuous manner?"

"Because this way his friends served as an alibi. Everyone thought the wife was already dead, so how could the husband be the murderer?"

"But didn't you search all the men when you arrived? What did Jennings do with the knife handle?"

"We didn't arrive until fifteen minutes after the 911 call. He had plenty of time to hide it." The detective paused as he composed a possible scenario. "The husband says he has to go to the bathroom, he cleans the handle, then he kicks it under his car when he meets us outside." The young man shrugged. "It could've been done any number of ways. But most importantly, it demolishes his alibi that he wasn't present at the time of death."

"But you haven't explained how the husband could enter a locked room. If I recall correctly, you said he had a key to the deadbolt, but the other two locks could only be locked from the inside."

"That stumped me, too. But then I figured it out. Dan Jennings has got to be the smartest murderer I've ever seen. I think he took a hammer and destroyed the two locks right after he KO'd his wife. Then, after he put the frozen blood on her, he simply closed the door and locked the deadbolt with his key — which was the only lock he hadn't already smashed. When they break in that afternoon, his friends believe they've broken all three locks, when in fact they've only broken one. The other two were already broken."

"Not bad," the pastor admitted, as he replayed the scene in his mind. "I assume you've queried the neighbors about the locks?"

"Why would I do that?"

"The noise, Mark. The *noise*. Surely if the husband acted as you believe, at least one neighbor would have heard him smash the locks that morning."

"Ahhh. . ."

The reverend sighed in mock reproach. But Mark was undeterred.

"Okay, I'll check it out. But even if they *didn't* hear it, it doesn't prove anything." The detective jingled the coins in his khakis as he thought of an explanation. "Maybe one neighbor had her TV turned up. Maybe another has bad hearing. Maybe another slept in late. Who knows?"

Nonetheless, Mark was annoyed that he'd missed such an obvious way to confirm his theory. Knowing his friend was chastising himself, Reverend Dean changed the subject.

"Let's move on. The lack of a head bruise bothers me. Plus, knocking a person unconscious is unreliable. How could Dan be sure Marie wouldn't wake up in *two* hours, instead of three?"

"Maybe he used a drug instead. That's more reliable, and after three hours it might have dissipated so much that we couldn't trace it."

"I like that better," the reverend agreed, as he dumped copious amounts of sugar in his coffee. "In fact, that part's probably true."

"Oh, you *agree* on that part, eh?" Mark asked, with equal parts amusement and annoyance.

Reverend Dean had to chuckle. "Well, I had to agree with you on something, Mark, or else you'd get discouraged," he teased. "However, I will say this, in all seriousness: it could have happened just as you describe. It would be an ingenious crime, and you don't surprise me by offering an ingenious solution. However, there are some incongruities."

"And they are. . .?" the detective asked warily.

"One, where is the stapler?"

"She didn't like the color! She didn't like the shape! She lost it!

The dog ate it! *Who cares?*"

The old man sighed, but continued.

"You segue nicely into the second incongruity. Why did the dog act as it did?"

"Randy Goodloe said he's never been in the unit, and we can't prove otherwise. But maybe he encountered the dog outside the building. Maybe he kicked the dog, or taunted it, or . . . who knows? Maybe the dog was just having a bad hair day."

Reverend Dean smiled as he gazed at the disheveled Puppadawg. He didn't think his four-legged friend had ever had a *good* hair day. Puppadawg looked at his master, knew he was thinking about him, and barked.

"Let's consider the unfortunate victim, then. Doesn't the position of the knife bother you?"

The young man sighed. "Not nearly as much as it bothered *her*," the detective rejoined. "Seriously, Reverend, she was stabbed in the heart. Where else would a knife *be* except her chest? Anyway, I have to go. I'll call you once we've interrogated him. I doubt this will take long, once he knows we've figured it out."

The minister stared at the coffee grounds in his mug and said nothing. Mark knew the old man was thinking, so he paused before hanging up.

Eventually Reverend Dean broke the silence. "Mark, is the apartment sealed?"

"Yes. Why?"

"I think . . . I think you should keep it that way. Just for now."

Mark was disappointed. He'd expected something more profound. "Fine. No skin off my nose," he agreed tersely. "I'll call you tonight."

* * *

Reverend Dean filled his mug a fourth time and descended to the den. His young friend was bright, and his solution made some sense. In fact, the reverend had considered this explanation himself when Mark initially described the crime. But he hadn't mentioned it for two reasons: one, he never took credit for an idea at the expense of another's ego. And two, well . . . it just didn't *feel* right.

But if not this way, then how?

Restless and still sick, he climbed back to his living room and peered out the window. As usual, the Matthews boys were playing baseball. As often as not, the oldest boy, Chris, hit the ball over the roof. The youngest boy, Seth, was lucky if he hit a ground ball into the bushes. He smiled at their nickname for him: Friar Tuck. He had to admit he bore a resemblance to that character, or at least to the actor who played that role in *The Adventures of Robin Hood*. It seemed—

Of course!

"What an idiot I am," he grumbled. Reverend Dean was rarely angry with others, but was merciless with himself. It was a habit Emma had tried, and failed, to break for decades.

"That would explain it *all* and I almost missed it!"

He shuffled to the kitchen and grabbed the phone. If he was lucky, he would be able to stop his friend from making a serious mistake.

"Small," answered a curt voice.

"Mark! I'm glad I caught you, I—"

"Reverend, you didn't catch me. I'm leaving right now. I'll call you later."

"Wait! Mark, I know who did it, and how it was done."

"So do I, Reverend. Remember?"

When necessary, Reverend Dean could be more imposing than his appearance suggested. He suppressed a cough and assumed his most authoritative voice.

"Mark, have I ever misled you?"

"Well, uh, not . . . that I recall, but—"

"My house is on the way to Jennings' store. Stop and give me five minutes. *Mark, this is important.*"

"Oh . . . all right. Five minutes."

It was unlike the reverend to act so peremptorily. But in a small town like Dark Pine, he knew an arrest would cause irreparable damage to Dan Jennings — even if he was vindicated. A cloud of suspicion would always hang over him, and his business and reputation would never recover. The pastor hurried to dress before his halfhearted visitor arrived. The doorbell chimed ten minutes later.

"Okay, Reverend," the detective said, barging in. "Five minutes."

"Where's your partner?"

"In the car." The young man thought it best to leave his partner in the cruiser. If Reverend Dean was wrong, there was no reason to broadcast the fact. If *Mark* was wrong, well . . . there was no reason to broadcast *that*, either. Reverend Dean instinctively understood. In fact, he agreed.

"Sit, my friend, sit." The minister motioned to the threadbare sofa. "There's no reason to stand, even for five minutes."

The young man reluctantly obeyed.

"Earlier, I mentioned three objections to your theory."

"We've already—"

"Now I would like to answer my own objections," he continued.

The old man raised a solitary, stubby finger.

"One," he began, "What does a stapler have in common with a pair of paper weights? Hmm?"

The detective gave an exasperated sigh. Obviously, he would

have to indulge his friend.

"Okay, they're both . . . office tools."

"What else?"

"They're both . . . hard. Unlike, you know, an eraser, or a cushion, or . . . whatever."

"What else?"

"They both might be the same color. Silver, gray or beige."

"What else?"

"Reverend, I've got a schedule, here."

The old man smiled in appeasement. "There's one other thing they have in common, my son."

He paused for effect.

"They're both *heavy*. Almost always, they're the heaviest items on a desktop. Was it a coincidence that the only things missing from the apartment were the three heaviest items in view?"

This got the young man's attention.

"Uh . . . you tell me," he replied cautiously.

"I also asked you about the behavior of the dog."

"Yesss," Mark agreed warily.

"You assumed I was referring to the dog's anger at Goodloe. I wasn't. Rather, I was referring to the dog's *tolerance* of *Astor*. Obviously, I expected the dog to accept Jennings. He owned the animal. And it was natural for the dog to growl at Goodloe, because he was a stranger. But why wouldn't he growl at Astor, as well? If neither man had been in the apartment, the dog shouldn't have known *either* man, and should have growled at both of them. Therefore, we must consider the possibility that Astor lied, and that he'd previously visited the loft."

Mark Small was glad that he'd left his friend in the car.

"Finally, I asked you to consider the position of the knife. More specifically, I referred to the *angle* of the knife."

The old man pointed to Puppadawg, lying supine on the floor

between them. The elderly St. Bernard was bigger than most children.

"Kneel next to Puppadawg."

"Reverend—"

"I just want to conduct an experiment. Go ahead, all he'll do is drool on you."

After making sure his partner couldn't view this spectacle through the window, Mark reluctantly kneeled next to the monstrous dog.

"Assume Puppadawg is the poor victim, and that she is unconscious and about to be stabbed. Pretend you have a knife. Show me how you would stab her."

The young man shrugged, wrapped one hand around an imaginary knife handle, placed another hand on top of the imaginary hilt, and used his weight to push the knife straight down into his "victim." Unaware he had been murdered, Puppadawg turned his ponderous head and licked the hands of his killer.

"Ah," beamed the pastor, "you would make an efficient killer. You used your weight, rather than mere arm strength, to push the blade into your victim. But that presents a problem, as I'm sure you see."

Annoyed, the young man *did* see. If the knife were visible, its hilt would be sticking out of the victim at a ninety degree angle — perpendicular to the floor — and not at the forty-five degree angle found in the woman.

"But the problem has an obvious solution," offered the pastor. "When would a victim be stabbed at a forty-five degree angle?"

Mark already knew the answer.

"If the victim and murderer were standing, facing each other," he replied. "The murderer thrusts the knife up from below, under the rib cage and into the heart."

"Just like what we have in Marie Jennings," the pastor said

quietly.

"So are you saying that *Astor* killed her? Jennings' assistant? But how? The D.A. won't indict someone just because a dog didn't bark. Particularly if we can't explain how he did it."

"Oh, I think we can do that," assured the reverend. "Mark, did you keep the apartment sealed, as I suggested?"

"Tight as a drum."

"Excellent. . ."

Abruptly, the pastor looked at his watch, arched an eyebrow and paused.

"So what's your theory? Don't keep me in the dark, Reverend."

"Actually, Mark, I think we've approached the end of your five minutes. I don't want to disrupt your schedule. . ."

"Okay, okay, I deserved that. Now *give*."

"Well, only if you're sure. . ." teased the pastor.

The detective gave what he hoped was a very official, and very stern, look.

The reverend smiled and cleared his throat.

"Very well then. Here's what I think happened."

Chapter 3

"I think that Jeff Astor is our murderer. I believe this for three reasons. One, the behavior of the dog. However, as you pointed out, that is circumstantial at best. The second reason is the knife angle. It simply doesn't fit with stabbing an unconscious victim.

"Third, according to you, Jennings was never alone when he worked in the yard. Moreover, our experiments with the knife angle make it unlikely that he killed his wife after he entered the apartment. Thus, since the M.E. indicated that the murder happened close to 1:00, we must eliminate Jennings as a suspect. So the murderer must be either Jeff Astor or Randy Goodloe. Yes?"

The detective examined the shine of his shoes. "Probably," he admitted, still looking downward.

The old man was grieved by Mark's dejection. It pained him to see his friend embarrassed in any way.

"Of course, even though Dan Jennings may not be our killer," the cleric assured him, "we would never have found the solution without the questions you posed to the crime lab."

Mark shrugged off the compliment.

"In fact," the reverend continued, "without the blood analysis — performed specifically at your request — we would be watching an innocent man go to prison."

The compliments seemed to have their desired effect, so the reverend returned to his analysis of the suspects.

"Proceeding under the assumption that the dog's behavior eliminates Goodloe, let's examine Astor. Unless I'm mistaken, he is an exceptionally evil man. It was Astor, you will recall, who suggested to Goodloe that they leave the room after they discovered the body."

"You're right. But why?"

"To leave Jennings with his wife, and thus destroy the alibi that he was never alone with her. In fact, I think he previously unplugged the kitchen phone to insure their departure. Astor is not merely evil, but smart; a highly undesirable combination. In fact, we can probably also add disloyalty to his list of vices."

"What do you mean?"

"He not only framed his employer for murder, but — unless I'm mistaken — he was having an affair with the victim."

"*What*!?"

"Think about it. It usually takes several visits for a dog to accept a person as a friend. Yet the German Shepherd completely ignored Astor the afternoon of the murder. Also keep in mind the 'cot,' as you called it, in the bedroom. I'm no expert on artist's lofts, but that makes no sense to me. Her home was just five minutes away. Why would she need a bed while she was working? I submit that naps had nothing to do with it.

"Finally, consider the locks. Most people have one lock, a few have two, but how many have *three* locks on their front door? Particularly when they don't sleep there at night? Not only that, but she habitually brought a German Shepherd with her as well. All this indicates that Marie was extraordinarily security conscious. Yet she nonetheless opened her door to the person who murdered her. If that person was not her husband — and you've established that no friend or neighbor ever visited — then who could it be other than a lover?"

"Well, once you put it that way. . ."

"It explains much, my friend," said the old man. "It also provides a second reason for the additional locks. It wouldn't be convenient for Dan to interrupt them *in flagrante delicto*, as it were. Of course, given Astor's actions, I believe we can safely assume that the relationship had soured. Which, if Marie was vengeful, meant that Astor's job was in jeopardy. And that gives us motive."

"But this is just speculation. The question remains, how did Astor — or anyone else — *do* it?"

"Ah, there I must give credit where it's due: to the Matthews boys, across the street. You know them, I believe?"

The detective rolled his eyes. "Reverend, what *are* you talking about?" he asked with exasperation.

"They play baseball almost every day. In fact, the eldest boy — Chris — frequently hits the ball over the roof of their house."

Mark's expression spoke volumes without a saying a word. The reverend came quickly to the point.

"The roof, Mark! That's the key! That's why I asked you to seal the apartment! Don't you see?"

The detective sighed — more from frustration than anything else — and looked at his sick friend.

"No," he stated bluntly. "I don't see anything."

Mark's partner honked the cruiser's horn from the driveway. Apparently he was becoming frustrated, too.

"Alright," acquiesced the pastor, "I'll run through what I think happened.

"Perhaps around 12:30, Astor separates from the other men and knocks on Marie's door. She answers; perhaps after he pleads that he wants to see her one last time. Whatever the excuse, she agrees to admit him and unlocks the door. He immediately stabs

Marie and lays her on the floor."

The pastor paused and changed subjects. "By the way, I assume it was Astor who volunteered for the painting chores that morning?"

"Actually, yes," Mark admitted, no longer surprised by anything the reverend said. "How did you know?"

The pastor shrugged. "A paint can would be a perfect place to conceal a bag of blood."

"Wait a minute. The blood was frozen, remember? Why are you calling it a *bag* of blood now?"

"Because it wasn't frozen when he poured it on her. It *had* been frozen — that's true — but that was only to mislead you."

"Mislead me *how*?"

"Why, son, in just the way you were misled. Before you could arrest Dan Jennings, you needed to explain how he could have killed his wife. That was impossible to do if Marie Jennings was dead when the men entered the apartment; because she died around 1:00, and Dan was never alone after 9:30. But if the blood was just meant to deceive, then that undermined the theory that the wife was already dead. Don't you see? It was the frozen blood that destroyed the husband's alibi, because there's only one reason you'd put frozen blood on the body: to mislead someone into thinking there was a wound. And if there wasn't a wound when the men entered the apartment, then *only* the husband could have killed her, because only the husband was alone with his wife after the men entered the loft. Astor created a crime with only one loophole — the frozen blood — and he relied upon *you* to find it, because that loophole would frame the husband."

"But how did Astor get her blood in the first place? He had to have it before he entered the apartment."

"He did. Do you recall that Marie underwent elective surgery last month? It's just a guess, but I'm assuming she gave some of her own blood to be used during the operation. It's a common practice, to insure that a patient doesn't receive contaminated blood from an anonymous donor. Perhaps Astor is a volunteer at the hospital. Or perhaps he bribed a worker at the blood bank."

"Okay, I'll check that out. But you still haven't told me how Astor killed the victim and left behind a sealed room."

"Well, all three locks on the door, of course, were simply locked by Astor after he entered the apartment and killed the unfortunate Ms. Jennings. He then removed his tarp—"

"*Hold it*," ordered the detective. "What tarp?"

"Mark, you've covered far more stabbings than I ever hope to witness, so surely you know that no one could stab another person — and leave behind all the blood you saw — without splattering some on himself. A murderer of Jeff Astor's caliber would have taken that into account, and put on a covering of some type — perhaps a thin, plastic poncho — just before entering."

The old man stopped and coughed for several seconds. This conversation was rapidly draining him. He didn't want Mark to notice, so he quickly continued.

"Think about it. If just one drop of blood fell on Astor's shirt, you would have immediately suspected him. That's why he probably wore gloves, too."

"But where's the *proof*? We searched all of them when we arrived, remember?"

"Ah . . . that brings us back to the roof. Once Astor stabbed Marie and poured blood on her corpse — hoping you would discover it had been frozen — he removed his poncho and went to the only place he could exit the apartment: the windows. He probably used a window in the last room — the studio — because it had windows which overlooked the front and back of the unit. At least I inferred that from your description. The other rooms were on one side of the unit or the other, thus offering a more limited selection. Am I correct?"

"Yes," sighed Mark. He didn't know if he was feeling ill because he was catching the flu, or because a housebound retiree understood the case better than he did.

"In any event, Astor opens the window that presents the best option of leaving undetected. As he hangs from the window sill, he slides the window shut, thus locking the mechanism. Consequently, it appears that the apartment has been locked from the inside."

"Okay, it's a good theory. Better than mine, even. But where's the—"

"I know, the proof. Remember the Matthews boys? Chris kept hitting the ball over the *roof*. What floor is Jennings' apartment on? The *top* floor. So where did Astor hide the poncho? On the *roof*, more or less."

"Reverend, there's nothing on the roof. We can see it from the street. There's nothing there. *Nada*."

The pastor smiled as he made his final suggestion.

"Well, of course not," he replied quietly. "But have you searched the gutter above the window?"

Mark's mouth almost opened. Although the apartment had been torn apart, no one had thought to search the outside gutter.

"I think," the reverend concluded as he placed a hand on his friend's shoulder, "that's where you'll find the poncho, and the stapler and paper weights which are holding it down."

Murder at the Fall Festival

Chapter 1

The old man poured his second mug of coffee, shook in prodigious amounts of sugar and nonfat powdered milk, and ambled to his study. Still bleary-eyed, he collapsed into a gray, cloth chair he'd purchased on sale at Wal-Mart, turned on his computer, and waited.

Reluctantly, the ancient monitor blinked on. One of the first things Thaddeus Dean did when he purchased the computer was select the "Mystery" theme for the computer's desktop. A spooky scene of a candlelit study with old bookcases now greeted him. He directed the cursor to a garish icon and double-clicked his Internet service provider's logo.

The Internet software on his computer was two versions out of date, but the old man didn't mind. He'd grown used to it, and the "welcome" screen wasn't as distracting as the newer versions which had constantly moving graphics. He wondered what that said about him. If he was younger, would he prefer constant motion on his screen? If so, was that good or bad? Did it indicate that younger users needed more stimulation to hold their interest, or that older users were more easily distracted? Probably both, he decided; and he feared that wasn't good news for either group. Mentally shrugging, he navigated to a screen which brought up a collection of news and sports.

After he updated himself on current events, he moved to a site where he'd customized a collection of that day's newspaper comic strips. The old man smiled through an assortment of twenty comics. Then he checked the weather. The next forty-eight hours predicted no rain, but the third through fifth days promised showers. That gave him something to look forward to. If it wasn't too cold, he frequently made himself a mug of hot chocolate, sat on his front porch and watched the storm approach. With the exception of a steam bath, it was his favorite way to relax. Especially if it was at night, when he could see God's fireworks: lightning.

Finally he checked his email. The old man received several pieces of spam — all braying that he could lower his mortgage or purchase hot stocks — but nothing from any friends. Disappointed, the retiree exited the Internet. He took a sip of coffee and stared at the candlelit scene on his monitor.

He was lonely and bored.

The loneliness had become an increasing problem for the old man. It began when his beloved wife, Emma, passed away. It became worse when he retired as senior pastor of Outpost Community Church. But this week was particularly bad, because his best friend, Mark — Dark Pine's youngest police detective — was on vacation in Las Vegas.

The boredom, on the other hand, was less common and more easily solved. His study — easily the old man's favorite room — held over a thousand books. He glanced at them and smiled.

One shelf held his collection of C.S. Lewis books; his favorite author. Several more held his collection of Bible commentaries. He had three commentary sets, in addition to a great many volumes on Christianity in general. Chuck Swindoll, Phil Yancey and Dallas Willard were well represented.

Emma's favorite authors, Francine Rivers and Joyce Meyer, were collected in a bookshelf near the study's door where she could reach them without disturbing him. He quickly looked away from that shelf.

Another bookcase — the reverend had eight in his study, each seven feet tall and overflowing — held popular fiction. Barry Eisler, Jeffery Deaver and Thomas Perry — with a smattering of Lee Child and Robert Parker — were assembled here. John Dickson Carr and Arthur Conan Doyle had bookshelves all to themselves.

The reverend was also interested in local, national and international history. In fact, one shelf was devoted purely to military history, and included *The Rise and Fall of the Third Reich*, *The Civil War: An Illustrated History* and a *Historical Atlas of the Napoleonic Era*.

But the cleric's interests spanned other topics, as well. As he glanced at another shelf, he saw books as diverse as *Prescription for Nutritional Healing* and *Art Deco Architecture*, to *The Complete Oil Paintings of Edward Hopper* and *Time and Religion*.

The reverend frowned. He couldn't recall reading that last book. Struggling up from his chair, he waddled to the sagging, particleboard bookcase and selected the volume. The old man was fascinated with time, and as he browsed through the book his boredom — and temporarily, his loneliness — soon vanished.

Chapter 2

The following day, Reverend Dean received a phone call at 9:30 AM.

"Reverend! This is Don Bracken! How are you this fine morning?"

The reverend doubted he really wanted to know. Don was a church deacon, as well as a good friend. In fact, he'd given the old man a ticket for a cruise last summer. Nonetheless, any disruption of the reverend's sleep routine — he invariably slept until 10:00 AM — was one of the few things that made him cranky. Particularly if the disruptor was cheerful.

Nonetheless, he sat up, took a deep breath and tried to sound civil.

"Uh, hello Don. I . . . suppose I'm fine. What can I do for you at this, uh . . . early hour?"

"I wanted to confirm my pick-up time, Reverend! To prepare for the Fall Festival! You're still going, aren't you?"

"Uh, of course, Don. I'm looking forward to it. How about," he stifled a yawn, "noon?"

"Great! I'll see you then, sleepyhead!"

Despite the early hour, the reverend appreciated Don's willingness to pick him up. Still, it didn't stop him from marveling at all the odd creatures God had created.

Jellyfish. Anteaters. Platypuses.

Happy morning people.

Suppressing a smile, the old man facetiously rebuked his Lord for the way he'd been awakened.

"That wasn't amusing," he said teasingly, pulling on a tattered terrycloth bathrobe. "That wasn't amusing, at all."

Minutes later, Reverend Dean sat on a worn sofa, slowly waking up. His right hand held a mug of coffee, while his left hand scratched the head of his elderly and massive St. Bernard, Puppadawg. It was Friday, and he reflected on the coming weekend.

Halloween was little more than week away, so — continuing a tradition he'd started almost twenty years ago — Outpost Community Church was organizing its Fall Festival. The Festival was always held the weekend before Halloween. Not so much to replace the holiday, but rather as a spiritual supplement to the event. The reverend knew that some Christians objected to Halloween completely — with its occasional emphasis on demons, gore and witchcraft — but Reverend Dean always enjoyed the holiday. He loved a good scare as much as — indeed probably more than — most people. In fact, he'd seen every Boris Karloff, Bela Lugosi and John Carpenter movie ever made. Still, he respected the opinion of those who disagreed with him, and completely understood their motivation. As a result, the Fall Festival was created to serve two purposes: a replacement for those Christians — particularly parents — who objected to the darker elements of Halloween, and as an annual gift to the community from Outpost Community Church.

The Festival would be considered modest by most towns, but positively large by Dark Pine standards. It had a variety of minor circus acts, including magic tricks, fire juggling and knife throwing; rides such as a merry-go-round, moon bounce and water slide; and various other activities such as water dunking, ring tossing and face-painting; all complete with candy prizes. The event had grown enormously since Reverend Dean first started it, and he was gratified at its popularity.

Unfortunately, its bigger size required more volunteers. That was why Don Bracken had taken a day off from work, and would soon arrive at the reverend's home. The Festival opened at 5:00 that evening, and ran until 10:00 PM the following day. Volunteers were asked to arrive as early as possible on Friday afternoon, in order to complete the banners, rake the grounds, set up booths and prepare the food.

Although the Festival itself was held on a vacant lot adjoining the church, the volunteers' "command center" was at the home of George and Tina Weston. The Westons weren't members of the church, but they were close friends of Tim and Maddie Brouchay, who were long-time attendees. In fact, both couples were part of a circus troupe that agreed to perform acts for the Festival. More importantly, the Weston's house was on the other side of the vacant lot, and — since their home was larger than the church — it provided a perfect base of operations. The reverend shook his head at the graciousness of the Westons. Either they had no idea of the turmoil about to engulf their home, or they were true saints.

After a third mug of coffee, the old man felt ready to tackle the world. He gave Puppadawg a final pat, leaned off the sofa, and ambled toward his bedroom to prepare for the day's festivities.

Chapter 3

Reverend Dean was gazing out his living room window when Don Bracken's red Honda pulled in the driveway. The old man motioned for Don to stay in his car, grabbed his jacket and locked the door. As he approached his friend's coupe, the reverend couldn't help but smile. He always enjoyed Don's company.

Even if their biological clocks only overlapped ten hours per day.

"Are you finally awake, Reverend?"

"Don, you won't be able to keep up with me," the old man teased.

Don recognized the source of the reverend's energy. "Ah. Coffee. Proof there is a God, and that He loves us."

The two men bantered throughout their twenty minute drive. Only as Don parked in front of the Weston's garage did the discussion turn to their duties for the day.

"I spoke with George on my cell before I picked you up, Reverend. No one's arrived yet, but they expect ten of us by 1:00. George and Tina will have the banners, paint, food and other items laid out by the time we arrive."

"They're very generous, but I'm afraid I've never met them."

"I met George through the Brouchays, and we're starting to

develop a good friendship. We've met for lunch several times, and speak regularly on the phone. He's a fascinating man. Do you know what he does for the circus? He's an escape artist. Lock him in a box, open it a second later and presto! He's in another box — or in another *room*. I've seen his act, and he's very good."

"I'm looking forward to it. What about Tina? What does she do?"

"I don't know her very well, but she handles knives. She throws 'em, juggles 'em and does tricks with 'em. If an act involves knives, she's your gal."

"Well, if Tina ever gets mad at George, he has a useful skill," the reverend joked. "Seriously, though, they sound like quite a couple. I can't wait to meet them."

The men approached the front door of the white, two-story, Colonial home. Seconds later Tina Weston opened the door.

"Hello, Don!" smiled a short blonde in her mid-thirties. After shaking his hand, she turned to the reverend. "And *you* must be Reverend Dean. I've heard a lot about you."

"I won't confirm it until I know what you've heard," the old man joked. "If it's bad then I'm Reverend Turner, from First Methodist."

"It's all good, I assure you," Tina laughed, inviting them in with a wave. "Except for Laurie, you're the first ones here. She beat you by five minutes."

An attractive brunette — the same age as Tina but six inches taller, with long, stylish hair — entered the room.

"Laurie, this is Don Bracken and Reverend Dean," introduced the hostess. "Laurie's an artist and family friend, so she volunteered to paint posters."

"Laurie Firpo," the woman smiled, looking nervously around the room. "Pleased to meet you."

For reasons the reverend didn't understand, Laurie seemed

preoccupied; almost nervous. But that could mean almost anything. She might be catching a cold, anxious about the oncoming horde, or just tired. Nonetheless, he filed his observation away for future reference.

"Gentlemen, if you'll lay your coats on the couch, I've got plenty of work for you to do. Laurie, the paint's in the garage, just inside the door."

Laurie returned with a can of paint, but looked unhappy. "I couldn't find a brush, Tina."

"Excuse me, Don, Reverend. I'll be right back."

Tina vanished inside the garage, returned with several brushes, then focused her attention on the men.

"Now let's discuss *your* chores," she smiled.

It was quickly apparent that George and Tina Weston had more to offer than just a well-positioned home. Tina, at least, was an excellent organizer. She had a flair for assigning tasks without appearing to order anyone around. Although Don was the nominal leader of the volunteers, he was more than happy to abdicate that role to Tina. As each volunteer arrived, the pert blonde assigned them an appropriate task and made sure the whole event ran smoothly. Don was ready to canonize her on the spot. Things were going so well, in fact, that by 3:30 Don, and a few others, had run out of things to do.

"Tina, I think I'm about done. Is George around? I don't think I've seen him today."

Tina frowned. "Well, he *was* outside putting the booths together, but I'm sure he's finished by now. Maybe he's in the garage, tinkering with his disappearing props. In any event, he's being anti-social. I'll get him."

Tina walked to the garage, tried the door and found it locked. Rolling her eyes, she returned to the kitchen and grabbed some keys.

"I locked it after I got the brushes," she explained on her way back to the garage. "George keeps his equipment in there, and he's paranoid that someone will find out how his tricks work."

Annoyed with the locked door as well as her husband's disappearance, Tina let herself in the garage.

Ninety seconds later everyone in the house heard her scream.

The reverend and Laurie were closest to the garage. They ran outside the house and immediately collided with a hysterical Tina.

"G-G-George! He's on the floor! I th-think he's *dead*!"

Reverend Dean handed the frantic woman to Laurie and quickly entered the garage. If George was hurt, it was more important to assist him than to comfort Tina.

A body was sprawled in the middle of the garage floor. Reverend Dean quickly knelt and touched the carotid artery. Nothing. Don joined him as he rose to his feet.

"Don, is this George?"

"Y-yes."

Over the years the reverend had seen his share of bodies. But he could tell by Don's expression that this was the first time his friend had seen a corpse. Since Tina was hysterical, he knew it was up to him to take charge of the situation.

"Don," he whispered gently, "we need to seal the garage and call 911. I'll handle the garage, if you'll keep everyone out and call the police. Will you do that?"

"S-sure, Reverend. Sure."

Don turned and walked slowly toward the house. Laurie escorted Tina to the living room, which temporarily left the reverend alone. He used that opportunity to examine the two-car garage.

The structure itself was attached to the house. It had no windows and just two entrances. The first entrance was the walk-in door, which was only three steps from the front door of the house. It was easily visible by anyone in the Weston's living room. The second entrance was a very large single door which allowed vehicles to enter the garage. It was the type of door which swung out as it opened.

The entire floor was solid concrete and — compared to the reverend's garage — was remarkably clean. Then again, he couldn't remember the last time he'd cleaned his garage, so that was somewhat relative.

The cleric craned his neck and looked at the ceiling. There were no rafters and no trapdoors leading to a loft. In fact, judging from the outside, there was no room for any type of attic.

Against the far wall of the garage there were several boxes — presumably containing George's disappearing props — along with a large, wheel-like structure. This puzzled him until he realized it must be a part of Tina's knife-throwing act. Along the wall adjoining the house were two free-standing, six-foot tall, metal cabinets. He walked to the cases and opened both doors. Although they were wide enough to hide someone, each held several shelves which were bolted to the cabinet walls. Only an infant could hide in these cabinets.

Lined along the closest wall were a work bench and various tool chests. Without consciously realizing it, he slowly nodded in satisfaction. The garage seemed normal in every respect. More importantly, none of the chests, cabinets or boxes were large enough to hold a body. Clearly then, George was not in the garage when Tina and Laurie collected the brushes and paint three hours ago. He must have entered during the last two-and-a-half hours, and via one of the two doors.

Actually, he realized, he could be more specific. In order to allow other vehicles to park in the driveway, Don had parked his car as close as possible to the main garage door. Although this main door couldn't be seen by anyone in the house, it was impossible to open it more than two or three inches due to Don's car. Nor could his vehicle be moved, because another car was parked behind Don's Honda. So George couldn't have walked, crawled — or been carried— into the garage from that door.

Consequently, he must have entered the garage via the walk-in entrance. Surely someone had seen him enter that door, together with whoever accompanied him. Satisfied with his analysis, Reverend Dean waddled outside the garage, shut the door without touching the knob, and entered the house.

Chapter 4

The police arrived minutes later. Since Mark was on vacation — and Dark Pine had only two detectives — Reverend Dean wasn't surprised to see the department's senior detective, Tom Michaels, stride into the house.

Reverend Dean had never met the man, although he'd occasionally seen him with Mark. The detective was middle-aged and slightly over six feet, with a square jaw, short blond hair and a large mustache. He didn't know if Michaels had ever served in the military, but it wouldn't have surprised him. If anyone looked like an ex-marine, it was Tom Michaels. Judging from his ring finger, he was also married.

Reverend Dean chastised himself as he touched the warm gold band around his own finger. More than anyone, he should know better than to jump to that conclusion. He had never removed his own wedding ring, although his beloved Emma had died over three years ago.

Shaking his head to dispel the encroaching sadness, the old man walked into the living room. Most of the volunteers were in the bedroom trying to comfort Tina. Deciding not to add to the commotion, he sank onto the sofa and waited. He knew that Michaels would consult with the patrolmen before meeting the volunteers. Ten minutes later, before speaking to any other witness, the detective approached him.

"So you're the famous Reverend Dean," Michaels began, with no hint of smile. "I've certainly heard *your* name a few times."

"Ah . . . hopefully in a positive light," the reverend countered.

"Oh, yes. Mark has made you quite a legend in the department."

The reverend smiled, but said nothing. It was obvious that Michaels didn't believe everything he'd heard.

"So you found the body," he continued. It was more a declaration than a question.

"No. I merely confirmed that George was dead, and then suggested that we clear the garage and wait for you."

"After you stayed there an extra minute or two."

The reverend shrugged and Michaels didn't pursue the point. The detective questioned Reverend Dean for another ten minutes, then asked a patrolman to usher Tina Weston and Laurie Firpo into the room. Reverend Dean remained seated.

"I think I'm done with you, Reverend," said the detective, obviously indicating the cleric should leave. "I know where to find you if I need you."

"Of course," the pastor smiled, rising from the sofa. "It was a pleasure to finally meet you, Detective Michaels."

"Yeah."

Reverend Dean waddled to the kitchen, puttered around the room looking for a glass of water, then ambled outside. However, rather than follow Michaels' suggestion, the old man spied a rocking chair on the back porch, pulled it close to the house and sat down. Meanwhile Tina and Laurie sat on opposite ends of the living room sofa. Tina was dabbing her eyes with a napkin, while Laurie was nervously eyeing Detective Michaels.

"First of all, let me say how sorry I am for your loss, Ms.

Weston."

There was nothing to say, so Tina merely nodded.

"I'll try to keep this brief. Reverend Dean filled me in on most of the details, so it seems obvious that your husband entered the garage through the walk-in door sometime after you and Ms. Firpo retrieved the paint and brushes. That was around 12:30, correct?"

Tina looked at Laurie for confirmation, and the lanky brunette shrugged in agreement.

"Yes," replied Tina meekly.

"Ms. Weston, as I understand it you were the organizer of this event."

"Just the afternoon preparations. Don Bracken was the overall coordinator."

"But inside your home, you told everyone where to go and what to do, right?

"Yes. I suppose so. I was trying to help."

"I understand that. I'm asking because I need to find out who saw your husband enter the garage. Who was stationed with a view of the garage door?"

Tina pondered the question.

"Well, I suppose Laurie had the best view, but there were several volunteers nearby, and they had a good view as well. Actually, I was next to Laurie most of the time — so that I could answer the door — but I never saw George."

"How about you, Ms. Firpo? Did you see anyone enter the garage?"

"No. Never." Laurie hesitated. "In fact . . . Tina, didn't you *lock* the garage door after you collected the brushes?"

"Oh . . . yes, I did." Tina looked up at the detective. "George . . . George is . . . was . . . concerned that someone might steal his tricks, so he warned me to . . . to—" The distraught woman couldn't continue, and began to sob. Despite his gruff appearance,

Michaels felt genuine sympathy for Tina. She was holding up better than he would. Laurie scooted over and hugged her friend. After a few minutes she composed herself.

"I'm almost done, I promise," soothed Michaels. "But I need to be clear. What you're telling me is that no one was in the garage when either of you went in at 12:30; that you locked the door after you left the garage; and that after you locked it, neither of you saw anyone enter the garage. Is that correct?"

Both women nodded.

"So . . . obviously George must have come in through the main garage door," deduced Laurie.

"No, Ms. Firpo, that's the problem. He didn't. Don Bracken's car was blocking that entrance the whole time." Annoyed and frustrated, Michaels stuffed his notebook in his shirt pocket.

"So how did he get inside the garage?" he asked no one in particular.

In an effort to solve that problem, Michaels fired a battery of questions to every volunteer in the house. But no one had seen George, or anyone else, enter or leave the garage. Sixty minutes later, finished with his interrogations, the detective walked into the kitchen.

"You can come in now," said Michaels, leaning toward the open kitchen window.

"Er . . . are you speaking to me?" asked the reverend. His eyes were wide with innocence, but his rocking chair was just six inches from the conveniently open window.

In response Michaels shut the window and left the kitchen. Reverend Dean sheepishly reentered the house.

"I saw you open the window when you got a glass of water. I trust you heard everything? Or should I have spoken louder?"

The reverend blushed a deep red.

"Ah, I do confess to being . . . concerned . . . by this afternoon's tragedy. After all, everyone in this house is a friend of mine."

"Even Tina Weston?"

"A recent acquaintance, granted, but I've known almost everyone else since the day they were born. I care deeply about what happens to them. Including what they may have . . . done to others."

"That makes two of us, Reverend. By the way, the M.E. should be in the garage by now. Since it doesn't have windows — and I don't want you bothering the doctor tomorrow — you may as well come with me."

Reverend Dean suppressed a smile, decided the less he said the better, and meekly followed the detective outside.

As they entered the garage a gentleman almost as old as Reverend Dean was kneeling on the floor, packing various pieces of equipment into a plastic carrying case.

"What have you got, doc?"

Dr. Jerome Frost snapped the case shut, then peered at the men through a pair of thick spectacles.

"Why, Thaddeus, what in the world are you doing here?"

Reverend Dean smiled. That solved one mystery. He'd wondered why Michaels thought he would talk with the M.E. tomorrow, and now he knew. The reverend and Dr. Frost were long-time friends.

"I could ask you the same question, Jerome. I didn't know you were Dark Pine's medical examiner."

"I'm not, usually. But Bud's in Seattle at some fancy forensics meeting, and I pinch-hit for him when he's gone. What's your excuse?" he asked good-naturedly.

"I happened to be in the wrong place at the wrong time, I suppose."

"That's the story of your life, Thaddeus. And you wouldn't have it any other way."

Michaels sighed. "I don't mean to *interrupt* the two of you, or anything" he intruded, "but there's a murder I need to discuss when you're through chatting."

Dr. Frost stood and looked at the detective with mock seriousness. "Well, if you *insist*, Tom," he smiled, winking at the reverend.

Michaels glared at the doctor, then pointed at the corpse. "When did he die, and how did it happen?"

The physician's smile vanished as he assumed a more professional air.

"The body is moderately warm and there's no rigor present. More suggestively, there's no lividity, and the internal temperature is 98.1 degrees." The doctor paused, and reflected on this information. "In my report, I'll say that death occurred between now and three hours ago. But between you and me, it was far more recent, almost certainly within the last hour."

Dr. Frost removed his glasses, cleaned them with a handkerchief, and considered Michaels' second question.

"Regarding how he died, you'll have to wait until Bud comes back on Monday for the autopsy. But the victim has a large contusion on the back of his head, and his eyes show classic signs of asphyxiation. My guess is that someone knocked him unconscious with a blunt object, and then suffocated him."

Chapter 5

Reverend Dean tried to speak with Tina before leaving, but she'd secluded herself in her bedroom. Consequently he waddled to Don's Honda, opened the door and squeezed inside. His friend was still talking with some volunteers, so that gave the old man time to think. He slouched deep into the seat and stared at the dashboard.

The conclusions of Dr. Frost, if accurate, were perplexing. If George Weston died within the last hour, then either Tina or Laurie was lying. Either one of them *entered* the garage, or one of them *saw* someone enter the garage.

The reverend dismissed the first alternative. Volunteers were constantly going in and out of the living room. He couldn't envision how either woman could enter the garage without someone seeing them.

He paused, propped an elbow on the door's armrest, then changed his mind.

Actually, there was *one* way: if Tina Weston and Laurie Firpo were acting together.

The cleric frowned. He didn't like it. That sort of conspiracy only happened in fiction. In real life, for two women to team up and kill someone was wildly improbable. For starters, he couldn't imagine a motive. What could possibly motivate George's wife to help Laurie kill George? Or vice versa? And even if such a scheme were true, how would they prevent a volunteer from walking in the room and seeing one of them enter the garage? In fact, the reverend himself had wandered through the living room several times, and neither woman seemed to care. He shook his head. That explanation made no sense.

He considered the second alternative. Did one or both women *see* George — and whoever was with him — enter the garage? Because at least two people *had* to enter the garage: George and his murderer. But that made no sense either. Both women knew there would be a constant flow of volunteers going through the living room. Even if they'd conspired together, they'd need to contact a third person — the murderer — and tell him the precise instant there would be no volunteers in the room. But that didn't seem possible. The flow of volunteers was too constant. More importantly, why murder someone in the garage in the first place? What was the point?

The cleric shook his head, sat up and saw Don Bracken approaching from the house. He didn't see how either woman could have participated in the crime.

But if not Tina or Laurie, then who?

Thaddeus Dean hadn't been home five minutes when his phone rang.

"Reverend? This is Don. I . . . I need your advice about something."

Reverend Dean was surprised. This was unlike his friend. However, Don had been unusually quiet during their drive home. The old man had attributed it to George's death, but perhaps it was something more.

"Of course, Don. What can I do for you?"

"Reverend, uh . . . Thaddeus—"

Now the cleric was alarmed. Although he had requested it many times, Don had never used his first name.

"Thaddeus . . . I have a question. Is communication between a confessor and a deacon privileged?"

The question surprised him, but it was an intelligent one, nonetheless. The concept of "priest-penitent" privilege meant that anything a confessor told a church leader — if said in confidence — need not be divulged in court. It was a longtime exception, because the state didn't want to infringe upon the ability of a person to honestly discuss his conduct with a pastor.

But more intriguingly, why had Don asked this?

"Don, you know I'm not a lawyer. But I doubt the privilege applies to deacons. I doubt it even applies to retired pastors. In our church, it probably only covers conversations with Titus," he replied, naming Outpost Community Church's current pastor, "and even then only in certain situations. Of course, I'm answering your question in the legal sense, not the moral one. What's troubling you, Don?"

"Reverend, George Weston called me last night."

Don said nothing else, and the reverend decided to wait until his friend was ready to continue.

"I haven't told you this — I haven't told anyone this — but George was having an affair. He . . . he was having an affair with Laurie Firpo."

Reverend Dean quietly pulled a chair from the kitchen table and sat down.

"But he was ending it, Reverend. He'd become truly contrite about his behavior and was going to stop seeing her. In fact, last night he left a recording on my machine saying that. At least . . . I *think* that's what he said."

"Don, I must warn you: whether you're covered by this privilege or not, anything you tell me won't be."

"I understand, Reverend. But I have to tell someone."

The cleric understood. "Since George is dead, it may not matter anyway. What did he say, Don?"

"He said, 'After talking with you last week, I found out something that makes it all moot. I've reached a decision. If she knew what it was, she'd kill me, but — '"

The reverend waited, but Don remained silent.

"But *what*, Don?"

"That's it, Reverend. That's all there was. I heard someone else enter the room, and apparently George didn't want that person to hear the conversation. I assume he was calling from home, so I suppose it was Tina. But whether he was talking about her, or whether he just didn't want Tina to hear about Laurie, I don't know."

"Don, you said you haven't told this to anyone. I assume that includes the police?"

"Not a word. I respect George's privacy and I don't want to hurt Tina."

The reverend approved of the motivation. Nonetheless, George's murder changed things.

"Don, I understand your reluctance. But we owe it to George to find his killer. I don't want to increase Tina's grief, but this might provide a motive for George's murder. Not just for Tina — if she knew about the affair — but for Laurie, too; because she might resent George for ending it. So since you're asking my opinion, I believe you have to tell this to Detective Michaels."

"Reverend, I . . . I've never done anything like this. Uh . . . look, could *you* . . . just take the cassette from my answering machine to the police?"

The reverend understood Don's fear of law enforcement bureaucracy. It could be intimidating.

"Don, of course I'll do it for you. But it's only delaying the inevitable. Detective Michaels will want to speak with you." He recalled his impression of the stern detective. "In fact, he'll *insist* on speaking with you."

"If he wants to, fine. But . . . to begin with, could *you* just take it to him?"

"Of course, Don. Bring it to me this evening, and I'll deliver it to Detective Michaels Monday morning."

Chapter 6

To the dismay of many, the Fall Festival was cancelled. The volunteers were in shock, but all agreed it would be an insult to George's memory to act as if nothing happened. After calling various people with the news, Reverend Dean sat down to a lukewarm supper in a dimly lit kitchen. He pushed his Hamburger Helper first one way, then another, then gave up altogether. Puppadawg, however, ate with relish. After licking his bowl clean, the massive dog cocked his head, looked at his master, then sat at the old man's feet. The reverend knew the dog was trying to comfort him, so he scratched the animal's head in gratitude. As the sun set, and the room gradually darkened, the two friends sat together in silence.

Forty minutes later, the reverend stood, walked to the window and peered at the evening sky. It was the worst possible combination. There were no rain clouds, but enough haze to block the stars. Disappointed, he walked to the living room. Finding nothing there, he walked downstairs to the den and debated starting a fire. Deciding it was too warm, he walked back upstairs and considered taking a steam bath. After removing his shirt, he decided he didn't want to do that, either. Finally, he went outside, started his old Ford, and drove to Wal-Mart.

The reverend had no real purpose in going to the store. He'd purchased groceries two days ago and rarely bought impulse items. Instead, he was going for a less tangible reason: he was lonely. He wanted to be around people, even if they were strangers.

The pudgy cleric parked at the edge of the parking lot, rather than near the entrance. He frequently did this so that he could get some extra exercise, as well as save a little wear and tear on the Ford. It took almost two minutes to walk to the store.

Upon entering, he had no particular destination, so he wandered. First the greeting card aisle, then the clothing section and eventually the grocery department. Starting with the boxed cereals, he ambled to the canned goods and finally to the frozen food section. Halfway down the aisle, he stopped in mid-stride.

He wasn't wandering at all. This was the route that Emma took.

First she read all the anniversary cards, eventually selecting one to give to him on their anniversary. They'd been married for decades, but she never forgot to give him a card on the date of their marriage. Not just every year, but every month. It was a rare financial extravagance for Emma, but one of the many small ways she expressed her love. Next, she looked at clothes, to see if there was anything they needed on sale. Finally, she shopped for groceries, always saving the frozen items for last, so they wouldn't thaw on the way home.

The reverend abruptly turned and left the store. He'd hoped that Wal-Mart would be a diversion until tomorrow's church service, but instead it depressed him terribly. He waddled to his dilapidated Ford, rested his head on the cracked steering wheel, and cried.

Chapter 7

After church the next morning the old man changed into his everyday clothes, ate a small lunch, then called Tina Weston. She'd declined Don's invitation to attend church, and he wanted to see how she was holding up.

"Hello?"

"Tina, this is Reverend Dean. I know you might not be in the mood to talk, but I wanted to see if there was anything I could do for you."

"There's . . . there's nothing anyone can do, Reverend."

"Would you like me to come over, my child?"

"N-no. I . . . I just want to be . . . by myself."

"We haven't known each other very long, Tina, but if George was anything like you, then he was a very special man."

This seemed to brighten the young woman.

"Oh, he *was*, Reverend! You would have liked him, and he would have liked you, too."

"Don spoke very highly of him."

"Did Don tell you that he loved pecan pie? I made it for him the first Saturday of every month. And he had a cigar every time the Seahawks played. And his favorite color was blue. And he loved to drive to the ocean. And . . . and . . . and Reverend . . . I'll never see him again!"

Tina wailed uncontrollably while the old man listened. As much as anyone, he knew what it was like to lose a spouse. Eventually the new widow regained her composure.

"I'm . . . I'm sorry, Reverend."

"There's nothing to be sorry about, Tina. Believe me, I understand what you're going through. Are you sure you wouldn't like me to visit?"

"I'm sure, Reverend. I . . . I have to go now. Thank you very much for calling. Good bye."

Tina abruptly broke the connection. The reverend slowly hung up the phone, got on his knees, and prayed for his newest friend.

Chapter 8

Early Monday morning — it was 11:00, but that was early for the reverend — the old man tugged open a rusty garage door, started his Ford and backed cautiously out of the driveway. He parked three blocks from Dark Pine's police station and carried a small package into the building. After announcing his arrival, he sat in the reception area and waited. Five minutes later he was escorted into Detective Tom Michaels' office.

It was small by most standards, but at least he had an office. Mark just had a cubicle. It was also bare to the point of being Spartan. But that fit Reverend Dean's impression of the man. Michaels was interested in facts, and he tolerated little sentimentality in the process.

"Reverend. This is certainly a . . . surprise," Michaels said, implying that it wasn't necessarily a good one. "What can I do for you?"

"I've come to talk about the case—" the old man started, but the detective cut him off.

"Reverend, look," he said, placing his forearms on the desk as he leaned forward. "Some people in this department think you can walk on water. But I'll be honest. I'm not one of them. I'm a trained professional. You're not. You're a *pastor*, for Pete's sake.

Despite what you see on TV, police work is specialized and complicated. I'm sure you're a very good minister, but in a criminal investigation, you're out of your depth. You have to leave this to the professionals."

Although he felt strongly on the subject, Michaels realized he may have hurt the old man's feelings. He tried to placate the reverend by giving him an example of what he meant.

"Take these photos, for example. You wouldn't know how to analyze information like this."

The reverend looked at several 8 x 10 color photographs spread across the detective's gray metal desk. They appeared to be the interior of a large bedroom.

"Well, Detective, since I don't know what you're trying to do, I'd have to agree. Perhaps if you told me exactly what you're looking for. . .?" the cleric replied, with a twinkle in his eye.

Michaels immediately realized that he'd made a mistake. He shouldn't have mentioned the pictures to begin with. But now that he'd brought them up, he had to explain them. In an effort to get rid of the old man, he gave a quick summary of the photos.

"They're pictures of a crime scene," he said curtly. "The victim had state-of-the-art locks on his bedroom door and a cell phone by his bed. Yet he opened his bedroom door in the middle of the night and walked straight into the arms of a burglar. So here's the question. Why would someone that security-conscious open his door — presumably because he heard a noise — rather than wait in his bedroom and call us?"

Reverend Dean was intrigued. To Michaels' annoyance, he stepped around the detective's desk to get a closer look at the photos. The pictures gave a three-hundred-sixty degree view of the room, including the floor, bed and most of the ceiling.

"This door leads to the bathroom?" the reverend asked, pointing to one of the photos.

"Yes. It's the master bath. So we know he didn't open the door to go to the bathroom, or to get a drink of water."

"Mmmmm. It *is* difficult—" the reverend began.

"See what I mean? This proves—"

"But I do have a suggestion for you."

The detective rolled his eyes. Surely his day could get no worse than this.

"Note the floor," the reverend began. "Do you see the bedspread? It's been thrown off the bed with no thought or order."

"Yeah? So?"

"Now look at the blanket. It's been tossed off, as well. Also in a disorganized fashion. But it overlaps just half the area of the bedspread. Thus, it was probably thrown off separately from the spread."

"So?"

"Now look at the sheet. It's not on the floor, but merely laid across half the bed; far more organized than the first two items."

"Reverend, look—"

"The important thing," the old man continued, "is that each item was removed separately. One at a time."

"Reverend, what's you *point*?"

Reverend Dean shrugged, then offered an explanation.

"It's just a guess, Detective — and a hasty one at that — but I think your victim was *hot*. First he threw off his bedspread, then he threw off his blanket, finally he pulled off his sheet."

The reverend pointed to the photographs.

"He might have had an expensive alarm system, but look at the walls of his room. There's no thermostat. All a burglar needed to do was enter his house, turn the thermostat to ninety, and wait until the owner opened his door to adjust the heat. Initially, when the burglar turned up the temperature, the victim didn't wake up. He merely tossed off his bedspread, and later his blanket, while half-asleep. Eventually, however, the heat fully roused him — which accounts for the more orderly condition of the sheet — and he rose to check the thermostat. That's why he opened the door. By the way," he asked sympathetically, "is this poor man dead, or comatose?"

Michaels was stunned by the old man's explanation — which no one had considered — as well as his question.

"Uh . . . why do you think he's either?"

The reverend shrugged as though the explanation were obvious. Which it was.

"If he could speak you'd be talking with him instead of studying these photographs. Thus he's either dead, or so disabled that he can't communicate with you."

The detective lowered his eyes and sighed. "He's dead. We believe he was hit over the head as soon as he opened the door."

Upon saying that Tom Michaels rose, walked past the reverend and closed his office door.

"Sit down, Reverend. Perhaps I misjudged you. Let's talk."

Chapter 9

Reverend Dean quickly updated the detective on Don Bracken's revelation. Unfortunately, after listening to the tape, it added nothing to what Don had said. As Michaels punched the eject button someone knocked on his door and — without waiting for a response — walked in. It was Dr. Frost.

"Well, Thaddeus, you're becoming quite a regular. Are you assisting Tom with this case?"

Michaels' face turned red, and Reverend Dean feared he was going to reply with more color than necessary.

"Detective Michaels has forgotten more about criminology than I'll ever know," he quickly replied. "He's merely humoring an old man, who's curious about a tragedy that affected his friends."

The doctor shrugged and Michaels' jaw relaxed.

"Whatever you say, Thaddeus. In any event, since you're 'curious,' you have good timing." The doctor plopped a file on top of Michaels' desk. "The autopsy report," he explained. "I was visiting Bud, and he asked me to bring it up. Do you want to read it, or do you want the condensed version?"

"Sit. Speak."

Reverend Dean smiled. He admired the detective's brevity.

"There's not much to tell," Frost replied. "Bud's autopsy

confirmed what I suspected at the scene. The deceased had been dead no more than three hours, but probably far less. He was rendered unconscious by a single stroke of a blunt instrument, then suffocated."

"Strangled?" Michaels asked.

"No. There were no finger or thumb marks, but there was a slight indentation circling his neck. Bud thinks a bag was placed over his head, and then tied around his neck to keep the air out. For what it's worth, I agree."

"Anything else?"

"Well," Frost shrugged, "to be honest, no."

"Okay, doc. Thanks for—"

"Er, I have a question, if I may," the reverend asked, looking at Michaels for permission. The detective gave the smallest nod possible, and Reverend Dean faced the doctor.

"Jerome, this is a question only a layman would ask, but would you explain why you're listing the time of death as a three-hour range, even though you believe he died during the sixty minutes prior to your arrival?"

"Actually, Thaddeus, it's a good question. But it requires a complicated answer."

The doctor leaned back, and laced his fingers behind his head.

"There are three main ways to determine death: rigor mortis, livor mortis and algor mortis. They roughly translate to: stiffness of death, color of death and temperature of death.

"Rigor is the one most people have heard of. When the body dies, it becomes limp. However, within four hours or so — give or take an hour or two — the body begins to stiffen. It begins with the smaller muscles — such as the jaw — then encompasses the larger muscles. This occurs due to the gradual disappearance of a substance called ATP. Of course, within a day or two, the muscle itself begins to break down, so the rigor disappears. There was no rigor present in George Weston. However, determining time of death by rigor is probably the least accurate of the three methods.

"Livor mortis is less well known. What it refers to is the discoloration of the body after the heart stops beating. When blood no longer circulates through the body, gravity takes over, and blood settles into the lower parts of the victim. After six to eight hours, this settling — or lividity — becomes fixed, and the blood stays in that part of the body even if the victim is turned over. Consequently, if someone is murdered while lying face-up, then turned face-down several hours later, we can tell that the body has been moved.

"Regarding George Weston, not only was it was too soon for lividity to become fixed, but his skin blanched when I touched it. Consequently, there was no lividity at all. After three hours, non-fixed lividity is almost always present, so that's one reason I believe the murder was committed closer to 3:00 PM than 1:00.

"To complete your lesson," the doctor smiled, "*algor* mortis refers to the temperature of the body. As you know, the internal temperature of a healthy adult is 98.6 Fahrenheit. After death, the temperature falls roughly 1.5 degrees per hour. Of course, this can be affected by ambient temperature, body weight, the clothing on the victim, and several other factors. But in any event, George Weston's internal temperature was 98.1, which—"

"Excuse me for interrupting, Jerome, but how is that temperature taken?" the reverend asked.

"Well, an oral temperature isn't reliable. Some M.E.s puncture a hole below the rib cage and insert a thermometer into the liver, but most smaller jurisdictions do what we do: take the temperature rectally."

Reverend Dean nodded and the doctor continued.

"In any event, an internal temperature of 98.1 suggests that the time of death was within an hour of my arrival. But let me be clear. There's an old adage which says that if an M.E. gives a precise time of death, then the police should arrest the *M.E.*, because only the murderer knows the exact time for sure. My point is that each of the methods I've described only provides a *range* to work with. I can give examples where each test has been wrong. I can even cite cases where the body temperature *rose* after death. That's why, to be completely accurate, I can only offer a three-hour time range for when this murder occurred."

"But you're not talking about one test," Michaels interrupted. "You said all *three* tests point toward the later time."

"Hence my unofficial conclusion," Frost replied.

Unfortunately, rather than pleasing Michaels, the doctor's conclusion merely annoyed him.

"But that doesn't *help*. It just makes things *worse*," said Michaels, throwing his hands in the air. "If you'd said that death occurred during the last *four* hours, then we have a suspect without an alibi: Tina Weston. If you'd said that death occurred during the last three-and-a-half hours, then that would include the time when Tina and Laurie were alone before Reverend Dean arrived." He shook his head in annoyance. "But you say that death occurred during the last *hour*; so everyone has an alibi, and we have no suspects. Because I've talked with every volunteer, and there was never a time when at least one other person wasn't with Tina Weston and Laurie Firpo."

Dr. Frost didn't know what to say, so he merely shrugged. Eventually, however, he spoke up.

"Well, Tom, the evidence doesn't lie. And in spite of my association with Thaddeus," Frost winked at Reverend Dean, "I still don't believe in miracles. So somehow you're going to have to explain how George Weston and his murderer entered a garage under the noses of three or more witnesses."

Chapter 10

On his way home Reverend Dean stopped by Dark Pine's library. It was small, held few books, and most if its furniture was childproof — and thus uncomfortable. Nevertheless, he visited the library even more than the bookstore.

One reason was the ILL — or Inter-Library Loan — system. In the reverend's opinion, it ranked second only to the printing press in terms of usefulness. It didn't matter whether Dark Pine's library had a book, because a patron could complete an ILL form and borrow it from another library.

He also enjoyed the library's magazine selection. The reverend couldn't afford many subscriptions, and buying issues at a store was even more expensive, so he kept informed by reading copies at the library. They'd even added *Christianity Today* at his request.

After spending a pleasant hour in an unpleasant chair, the reverend headed home. It was still a few hours until dinner, so he shuffled to his study, picked up *Time and Religion*, and continued where he left off.

Ten minutes later the old man set the book gently on his lap. It wasn't telling him anything new. He realized that western man viewed time in a linear fashion, while many in the east viewed time as circular. Given such a perspective, it was easier to understand the eastern belief in reincarnation. It wasn't a Christian concept,[9] but it was fascinating nonetheless.

But that wasn't why he put the volume down. The book's picture of a wheel — representing the eastern view of time — triggered something in the back of his mind. The reverend knew it was important, but he couldn't pluck it from his subconscious. Fortunately, he knew what to do.

Stop thinking about it.

The old man closed the book and grabbed a sheaf of papers from the corner of his desk. They were a hodgepodge of newspaper articles, magazine pages and email printouts, all discussing books which appeared interesting. He clipped the information from each piece of paper, then dropped the cutouts into a brown, cardboard folder. Each month he reviewed the items in the folder, filled out ten ILL forms — the maximum allowed — and presented them to the reference librarian for action. He was sliding the tattered file back in its cubbyhole when it hit him.

He knew why the circle was important. But that only solved half the problem. What about—

Then the old man remembered the murderer's occupation. It was bizarre, but it fit. It all fit.

The reverend knew he would have a hard time convincing Tom Michaels of his theory. He needed proof, and he knew just where to get it: Wal-Mart.

The old man backed carefully out of his driveway, but once on the road he coaxed his ancient car to the speed limit; a rare occurrence for the reverend. Arriving at Wal-Mart's parking lot, he even parked next to the main entrance. Upon entering, he looked around and planned his expedition.

First, a cigar. Not the cheap ones in a wrapper, but an expensive one in a metal tube.

Next, the women's section. He needed a curling iron. The reverend felt distinctly out of place, because balding men rarely used curling irons, but finally he decided on a pink, half-inch model. Next, the—

"Well, Reverend," observed Tom Michaels, looking at the cigar, "I didn't know you smoked."

"Oh . . . hello, Detective. I, ah . . . don't."

Michaels looked at the curling iron.

"I'm tempted to ask if you use *that*, but I'm not sure I really want to know," he smirked. The detective was clearly enjoying himself.

"Ah, that's not really . . . for me, either," blushed the reverend.

"Well, *I* only came to buy beer. But I have to admit, Reverend, your trip's a lot more interesting. Can I help you carry anything? I can't wait to see what you're getting next."

The old man liked a good tease better than most, but this had gone on long enough. "Actually, Detective, you *can* help me. In fact, I plan to share all this with you. Will you be home this evening?"

"Ahh . . . actually, Reverend, I was just joking. It's obvious that you don't need—"

"I'll call later tonight, then," smiled the reverend. "Until then, Detective."

Michaels watched the old man waddle into the sporting goods department, very much wishing he hadn't said anything.

The reverend had mixed feelings on the way home. He couldn't really afford his purchases, but there was no other way to test his theory. He resigned himself to no banana pudding for the next two months; a very high sacrifice for the cleric. Once home, he spread his purchases across the kitchen table, rummaged around for a meat thermometer and began his experiments. An hour later, satisfied with the results, he sat down to finish his leftover Hamburger Helper. Emma once told him that a balanced meal always included vegetables, so he opened a can of spinach, sat it next to his plate, and ate it with his meat and pasta.

Then he called Tom Michaels.

"Detective Michaels? This is Thaddeus Dean. Did you find the beer you wanted?"

Until now, Michaels had desperately hoped the reverend wouldn't call.

"Er, yes, Reverend."

"Have you eaten dinner?"

"Ahh, yes. . ."

"Good. Would you like to know how George Weston was murdered?"

"You know?"

"Yes. But to prove it, we need to go on a . . . what's the word . . . a stakeout."

"Reverend, look. . ."

Michaels was going to explain that he'd just opened a Coors, removed his shoes, and was relaxing in front of a Sonics game. Instead, he opted for a more direct reply.

"No."

Anticipating this response, the reverend used the only leverage he had with Michaels. Fortunately, it was potent.

"If you do, and I'm wrong, I'll never bother you again."

This welcome prospect caught Michaels off-guard.

"Promise?" he said eventually, and guardedly.

"Promise."

"Remember, you're a *reverend*. . ."

"*I promise*, Detective."

"Fine. I'll see you in fifteen."

* * *

Thirty minutes later Michaels cut his lights and quietly parked one block north of Tina Weston's front lawn.

Sixty minutes later the inside of the car had grown cold, and Tom Michaels' temper had grown hot.

"Are you going to tell me what this is all about?"

"I'd prefer to wait, Detective. If I'm wrong, you'll think me a fool."

"I hate to break it to you, Reverend, but I'm *long* past that—"

Suddenly the cleric sat up.

"There she is! Do you see what she's doing?"

Michaels squinted through the darkness.

"She's . . . she's taking out the garbage."

"Exactly! Now she's gone back inside. We can pick it up."

"We've been waiting for garbage?"

"It's perfectly legal, Detective. However, I suggest we take it to my house. I'm sure your wife is a fine woman, but I doubt she'd appreciate garbage strewn throughout her living room."

Chapter 11

Upon seeing a blue tarp spread across the reverend's living room floor, Michaels realized the old man had been one step ahead of him the whole time. He threw the bags on the floor in disgust.

"I'm not doing anything — and I'm *certainly* not going through someone's garbage — until you tell me what you're doing."

"What we're doing, Detective, is looking for any, or all, of the following: an unused cigar, the metal tube it came in, pieces of an ironing board cover — or perhaps pieces of a lampshade — a curling iron, oven mittens . . . and perhaps one of those knee or back wraps that produce heat when exposed to air. One of those reflective, metallic space blankets would be helpful, too. You know, the kind that looks like aluminum foil."

The old man paused, then held a finger in the air.

"And an immersion heater. Perhaps you've seen one. It's a coiled aluminum rod, about four inches long, attached to an electric cord. You plug the cord in the wall, and immerse the coil in a cup of coffee to heat it. Sometimes it's called a heating coil."

Michaels looked at the old man as though he had lost his mind. "That's it. I'm out of here."

The detective walked toward the kitchen door.

"And while we're looking, I'll explain how Tina Weston

murdered her husband."

Michaels paused, took his hand off the doorknob and walked back to the living room.

"*You* talk. *You* rummage. *I'll* listen," he said, sitting on the sofa.

"Of course, Detective."

The old man emptied all three bags of garbage on the tarp, dropped to his hands and knees, and began sorting.

"We have a motive," Reverend Dean began. "Tina apparently discovered that George was cheating on her. Now we just need to find out *how* it was done."

After picking up a banana peel, followed by a messy can of split-pea soup, the reverend grabbed the corner of the sofa, pulled himself up, and vanished inside the kitchen. Seconds later, he returned with a box of resealable plastic bags and a pair of disposable gloves.

"You'd be surprised how useful these are," the reverend commented, as he snapped the elastic gloves over his hands. "Anyway, where was I? Ah . . . how it was done. As you know, the biggest problem was the time of death. Jerome explained that quite well, I thought. Remember the three terms? Algor mortis, livor mortis and rigor mortis.

"Rigor we can dismiss out of hand. As Jerome explained, it's the least reliable way to determine time of death, and it doesn't rule out the possibility that death could have occurred before Don and I arrived.

"Livor is more difficult to explain. As you'll recall, that's where the time of death is determined by bodily fluids settling into the lower portions of the body."

The old man scanned the tarp, trying to remember where he left the split-pea soup. After finding it he got on his hands and knees, tossed it into a far corner of the tarp, and resumed his search.

"By the way, Detective, did I mention that the subject of time fascinates me? No? Well, it's interesting that certain eastern religions view time in a circular manner. In fact, in a book I'm reading, the author uses a wheel to describe how a person ostensibly enters a new incarnation. Then a thought occurred to me: if a wheel can usher in a new incarnation, could it not seemingly *postpone* a departure, as well?"

Michaels had no idea what the reverend was talking about, but as long as he didn't have to sort trash he was willing to let him ramble.

"Speaking of wheels," the reverend continued, "there's a large wheel in the Weston's garage. Do you know what it's used for?"

"Ahh . . . it's part of her knife-throwing act, isn't it?"

"Indeed. An assistant is strapped to the wheel, and Tina hurls knives at that person while the electric wheel spins in a circle."

"So?"

The cleric rose to his knees and peered directly at the officer.

"Detective Michaels, if a body was strapped to that wheel, and the motor turned on so that it rotated very slowly, wouldn't that prevent bodily fluids from settling?"

Michaels' mouth literally fell open. The reverend, however, bent back down and resumed sorting.

"That leaves us with algor mortis," the old man continued, tossing aside an empty tuna can. "As you'll recall, that's internal body temperature. A healthy body is 98.6 degrees, and George Weston was 98.1 when Jerome took his temperature. Since internal temperature falls roughly 1.5 degrees per hour, that presented a problem." The reverend pulled a small object from the pile of refuse. "Until now."

With some pride, he held up a new, unused cigar.

"Why would Tina throw away a perfectly good cigar?

Particularly one as expensive as this?"

Michaels shook his head.

Very carefully, the reverend inserted his small finger into an empty cigar tube, and held it up for Michaels' inspection.

"To use this, of course."

Walking on his knees, the old man shuffled to the edge of the tarp, grabbed a resealable bag and dropped the tube inside the plastic. After sealing the bag he resumed his search.

"How can an internal rectal temperature be altered? I apologize for being distasteful, but there's one obvious way: by inserting something warm into the cavity. Hence our search for items that produce heat. But therein lies the problem. Every item I've examined produces a *lot* of heat."

The reverend rose from the floor with a grunt, waddled into the kitchen and returned with the items he'd purchased at Wal-Mart.

"Take this immersion heater. It's the star of the group, and generates two hundred degrees of heat. Or this curling iron. Even at its lowest setting, it emits one-hundred-forty degrees; at least according to my meat thermometer. Even this disposable hand warmer is too warm. I didn't measure it, but its wrapper claims that it averages one-hundred-thirty degrees."

The old man paused to let Michaels digest this information.

"Now, I realize that Jerome said the temperature of a body can, very rarely, *rise* after death, but surely not to one-hundred-thirty degrees. How could Tina use one of these items, yet still produce an appropriate temperature? Let's try to find out."

The cleric rummaged in the trash for several more minutes, then — with a grunt of satisfaction — held up two items.

"Do you know what this is?" inquired the reverend, extending one of the items closer to the sofa.

"A piece of cloth, obviously," replied Michaels. "Gray on one side, white on the other. Maybe . . . six by six inches. You tell me. What is it?"

"I believe it's part of an ironing board cover. As you know, it's highly resistant to flame. And this," said the reverend, holding forth his other hand, "is obviously a curling iron. This specific iron has several admirable features. The heat is adjustable, the cord has an anti-tangle feature, it has a small diameter, and it's a travel model; so it can be folded for easy concealment. In fact, having compared various models at Wal-Mart, with some, ah . . . helpful guidance from you," the old man glanced at Michaels with a smile, "I can say with confidence that an iron with all these features is quite uncommon."

Michaels rolled his eyes but said nothing.

"In any event, if we wrap the ironing board cover around the curling iron, like so. . ." the cleric's actions mimicked his words, "it provides admirable insulation. More to the point, it reduces the heat emitted by the curling iron. Inserting this into a cigar tube lessens the heat even further. I won't slide it into the tube, because you'll want to send that to your lab. However, once it's analyzed, I believe you'll find fecal matter on the outside of the tube. I don't know if that will produce usable DNA, but — if not — you may find traces of paint from the tube inside George Weston's rectal cavity. Absent that, you may find, ah, that the heat. . ."

"'The heat' what?"

The reverend had no difficulty discussing lividity and other topics, but he was slightly uncomfortable with this suggestion.

"Ah, the heat may have slightly . . . cooked . . . that area."

Michaels screwed up his face. Partly in disgust, but mostly because the cleric was thinking of things that should have occurred to him.

"But why kill him in a way that's so easily detectable?"

"When the cause of death is obviously suffocation, most small-town M.E.s don't see a need to closely inspect the rectal cavity. And to be on the safe side, I'm sure that Tina planned to cremate him as soon as possible."

The old man shook his head, out of regret more than anything else, and changed the subject.

"By the way, in case you were wondering, we were searching for pieces of a lampshade and/or oven mitt because those items might have been used in lieu of an ironing board cloth. The metallic blanket, if it was used at all, reflected George's heat back to his body, thus minimizing his exterior temperature loss. That way, Jerome wouldn't notice a discrepancy between the internal temperature and how the body felt to the touch. It's better than an electric blanket, because that would have sped the onset of rigor. Perhaps you'll find one in her home."

The old man scanned the floor to see if he'd missed any other evidence. Deciding there was nothing of interest, he pulled off his gloves, tossed them into the middle of the tarp, and plopped into a nearby chair.

Michaels was alternately intrigued and perplexed. "So you're saying. . ." he began, not knowing where to start, "so you're saying that . . . Tina Weston and Laurie Firpo were in this together? I mean, Laurie went inside the garage, and then claimed that she didn't see anything; so she must be in on this with Tina."

"Not necessarily. In fact, I believe Laurie is innocent." The old man suddenly recalled Laurie's adultery. "Of George's murder, at least. In any event, here's what I think happened: Tina lured George into the garage before Laurie arrived, and knocked him unconscious. She then tied a bag around his head to suffocate him. She killed him via suffocation — rather than hitting him again — because congealed blood around a wound would have fixed the time of death; as would eye dryness, so she closed his eyes as well.

"She then strapped him to the wheel and turned the wheel

toward the garage wall. As a result, Laurie only saw the *back* of the wheel when she entered the garage to get the paint. Tina also intentionally hid the brushes. So when Laurie said she couldn't find them, Tina had an excuse to return to the garage. At that point she inserted the curling iron and turned on the wheel. On her way out she locked the door so that no one else could enter."

Trying not to grimace, the old man readjusted his posture. Crawling on the floor had caused his back to spasm.

"And, of course, I'm sure you immediately noticed the anomaly when Tina returned to the garage almost three hours later."

Michaels hadn't noticed anything unusual, but refused to admit that to the reverend. Instead, he sagely nodded his head.

"I was confident you would. As you pointed out, that's why you're the detective, and I'm the minister. Because the fact that Tina didn't scream for almost ninety seconds after reentering the garage escaped me at first. I believe that's when she unstrapped George's body from the wheel, pocketed the curling iron, and hid its extension cord. As I mentioned, this particular iron has a cord that spins three-hundred-sixty degrees, so it didn't tangle. That's how it could function even though the wheel rotated."

The old man paused out of a small degree of admiration. He was frequently conflicted between his respect for a well-crafted plan, and the evil which prompted it.

"We're fortunate that Tina didn't take more time to prepare this murder. She obviously used whatever materials she found in her home, whereas other items would have been more effective and harder to trace. Thus, it was clearly planned on the spur of the moment. The mind that could produce this scheme, in such a limited time, is frightening.

"However, it's . . . unusual . . . that she killed George the day *after* discovering his adultery. I could understand — though obviously not condone — killing in a fit of passion as soon as she found out. And, given her intellect, I could envision Tina biding her time and planning a murder that would be hard to detect. But I'm perplexed why she killed him the next day."

Michaels shrugged. "It might be about something else. You heard the tape. George didn't even mention his relationship with Laurie Firpo. He just said that he'd learned something which made everything moot."

The cleric nodded.

"That's true. There may be an unknown reason. Perhaps you'll find out when you arrest her."

The old man peered at Michaels, then swept an arm over his garbage-strewn floor.

"Assuming all this has been convincing?"

It had been very convincing. But Michaels wasn't ready to admit it.

"Uh . . . let's see what the lab says about the cigar tube. I'll also order a closer exam of George Weston's body. If the tests bear you out, well . . . we'll see."

Although Reverend Dean had nothing more to add, Michaels remained seated. The detective was uncomfortable in the role of supplicant, but there was one question his curiosity forced him to ask.

"Ah, I do have . . . a question, Reverend," Michaels began hesitantly. "I understand how seeing a wheel helped you solve the livor mortis problem. But what made you think of the curling iron? They aren't related at all."

The old man smiled.

"Ah, but they are, Detective. Tina Weston performed all manner of tricks with knives, did she not? She threw them, juggled them . . . I'm even told she swallowed them. When they were on *fire*, mind you. Imagine that: swallowing a flaming sword."

"So? That's not uncommon. How did that tip you to what she did?"

"Well, not to be indelicate, Detective, but surely it doesn't take much imagination to appreciate that if hot metal can go in one end, it can also go in . . . the other?"

Two days later, Dark Pine's senior detective called Reverend Dean.

"Well, the lab agreed with you, and we arrested her this morning. She denied everything, of course, but get this. Do you remember the photos you saw on my desk of the man who was murdered during a burglary? We found items from his home in her attic. I think what George learned was that his wife was augmenting her income by burglary. Presumably he didn't approve; particularly when it included murder. I think George was going to turn her in after the Festival, and *that's* why Tina murdered him the next day. She probably didn't even know about his affair with Laurie."

Reverend Dean considered this information. "I agree, Detective. That makes a lot of sense. I see again why Mark speaks so highly of you."

Michaels' silence indicated that he wasn't finished with the conversation. He clenched his jaw and unconsciously lowered his voice to a whisper.

"Still, I . . . I suppose I'm in your debt."

Reverend Dean knew this was difficult for Michaels to admit. However, it had never been his intent to upstage anyone. He'd merely wanted to help his friends.

"Detective, you are no more in my debt that I am in yours. Without your help, none of this would have been possible. The credit is yours, and I insist that you take it."

It was typical of the old man to commend others when he'd done most of the work. But he didn't see it that way. He attributed his powers to the Lord, and to take credit for them would be like taking credit for the sun or the rain.

It was at that moment that Tom Michaels realized he was speaking to a very special man.

Chapter 12

It was twilight and the weather predictions were accurate. Thunder clouds were rolling in from the west. The reverend smiled, mixed a mug of hot chocolate, and ambled onto his front porch. Puppadawg knew exactly what his master was doing, and followed the old man outside. The massive hound sat on a blanket next to the reverend's chair, and rested his huge head on his paws.

Reverend Dean lived at the end of the street, so his only neighbors were to the west. He casually scanned the closest homes. The Matthews lived across the street. He could tell by sounds coming through their open window that the parents, Shirley and Pete, were having dinner with their young sons, Chris and Seth.

Phil and Joyce lived adjacent to the reverend. Their window was closed, but the reverend could see Joyce speaking on the phone while stirring something in a pot on the stove. The only other home in view, next to the Matthews, was owned by Abe and Rebecca Cohen. Judging from the silhouettes behind their kitchen blinds, they too were sharing dinner.

The old man remembered how much he enjoyed eating supper with Emma. For decades he took that small joy for granted. He hoped his neighbors appreciated how wonderful, and how temporary, that joy could be.

Then he scratched Puppadawg, took a sip of hot chocolate, and watched the rain approach.

ENDNOTES

Page numbers refer to the pages in this book.

[1] Luke 16:19-31. (Page 10)

[2] Pictures of the *Kalakala* can be viewed at www.kalakala.org. (Page 16)

[3] Jude 13. Also see Matthew 8:12, 22:13, 25:30; 2 Peter 2:4; and Jude 6. (Page 107)

[4] E.g., John 1:4-9, 3:19, 8:12, 9:5, 12:35-36; 1 Peter 2:9; 1 John 1:5; and Revelation 21:23. (Page 107)

[5] As Dostoevsky speculated in *The Brothers Karamazov*, "... I believe that if the fire was physical, sinners would be glad, for if they were subjected to a physical ordeal, they would forget for a brief moment the infinitely more fearful spiritual torment." (Bantam, 1970). (Page 107)

[6] Hebrews 13:2. (Page 143)

[7] See, e.g., *Rare Earth*, particularly the final two chapters, by University of Washington astrobiologists Peter Ward and Donald Brownlee (Copernicus, 2000). (Page 154)

[8] It is estimated that this syndrome affects up to 15% of the population, and manifests as a very unpleasant, creepy-crawly sensation in one or more legs, accompanied by an almost irresistible urge to move the affected limb. It occurs only when the body is at rest, and (without medication) can only be relieved by moving the affected leg. A related disorder, Periodic Limb Movement Syndrome, causes frequent leg jerking — as often as

every 20 seconds — during sleep. The former prevents a sufferer from falling asleep, while the latter prevents a deep, restorative sleep. More details can be obtained at www.rls.org and www.wemove.org. (Page 174)

9 Hebrews 9:27. Reincarnation is also associated with the concept of "karma," which teaches that a person's next life is determined by the conduct of his current life. This cycle continues until the person becomes sufficiently righteous. Thus, as one Tibetan Buddhist wrote, "Our destiny is in our own hands." This clearly differs from the Biblical assertion that man cannot save himself by his own works. (Page 236)